Nicole ❀ 'Dell

DARE TO BE DIFFERENT

Interactive Fiction for Girls

Other books by Nicole O'Dell

Risky Business
Swept Away

Nicole O'Dell

DARE TO BE DIFFERENT

Interactive Fiction for Girls

BARBOUR
PUBLISHING

Published by Barbour Publishing, Inc., P.O. Box 719, Uhrichsville,
Ohio 44683, www.barbourbooks.com

*Our mission is to publish and distribute inspirational products offering
exceptional value and biblical encouragement to the masses.*

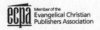 Member of the
Evangelical Christian
Publishers Association

Printed in the United States of America.
Bethany Press International, Bloomington, MN 55438; March 2011; D10002724

TRUTH OR DARE

DEDICATION

*This book is dedicated to my mom, Carolyn, who
cried when she read it. I never understood, until
I became a mother myself, how much heartache
could come from watching a child face important,
life-altering decisions. Mom, your long-suffering
faith in God and unconditional love for me inspire
me as a mother and a writer to make the
decision-making process easier for young girls.
I love you, Mom.*

Chapter 1

RULE THE SCHOOL

The first bright yellow light of day peeked through the blinds covering her window. Lindsay Martin stretched and yawned as she slowly woke up. Having tossed and turn much of the night, she was still sleepy, so she turned over and pulled the puffy pink comforter up to her chin and allowed herself to doze off for a few more minutes, burying her face in the coolest spot on her pillow.

But wait! Lindsay sat up quickly and threw back the covers, remembering that it was the first day of school. She jumped out of bed.

She had carefully selected her clothes the night before; the khaki pants and screen-print tee were still hanging on her closet door, just waiting to be worn. But now they seemed all wrong. Frantically plowing through her closet for something different to wear, Lindsay pushed aside last year's jeans and T-shirts and found the perfect outfit: not too dressy, not too casual, not too anything. As an eighth grader, she wanted to look cool without looking like she was trying too hard— the fashion kiss of death. Confident that she had selected the perfect outfit, she padded off to the bathroom to get ready to face the day.

Happy with how she looked—jeans with just the right amount of fading down the front, a short-sleeved T-shirt layered over a snug long-sleeved T-shirt, and a pair of sunglasses perched atop her blond hair—she bounced down the stairs, slowing as she reached the bottom. Lindsay sighed when she recognized the smell of bacon coming from the kitchen. "Mom, I'm really not hungry, and I have to go meet the girls!"

"Now you know I'm not going to let you head off to school without breakfast, so at least take this with you." Mom held out Lindsay's favorite breakfast sandwich: an English muffin with fluffy scrambled eggs, cheese, and two slices of bacon.

Lindsay wrapped it up in a napkin so she

could take it with her and gave her mom a quick kiss before rushing out the door. "Thanks, Mom. You're the best!"

Hurrying toward the school, Lindsay munched on her sandwich along the way. Nerves set in, and halfway through her sandwich, her stomach rebelled; she tossed what was left into a nearby trash can, where it fell with a thud.

After her short walk down the tree-lined streets, she arrived at the meeting spot—a large oak tree in the front yard of the school—about fifteen minutes early. Shielding her eyes from the sun and squinting, Lindsay watched the street for the first sign of her three best friends. She expected Sam and Macy to arrive by school bus—they lived too far away from the school to walk. Kelly lived close enough to walk, but her mom usually dropped her off before heading to her job as an attorney in the city. Lindsay was thankful that she lived so close to the school. She loved being the first one there to greet her friends each morning. Since her mom didn't have to leave for work, and Lindsay didn't need to catch the bus, she had a bit more flexibility and could save a spot for them under their favorite tree.

The bus pulled into the driveway, squealing as it slowed. It paused to wait for the crowd of students to move through the crosswalk. When it finally parked, the doors squeaked open and students began to pour off the bus just as Kelly's mom pulled up to the curb right in front of Lindsay.

"Bye, Mom!" Kelly grabbed her new backpack out of the backseat and jumped out of the car. At almost the same time, Macy and Sam exited the bus after the sixth and seventh graders got off.

Excitedly the four girls squealed and hugged each other under their tree, never minding the fact that they had been with each other every day for the entire summer. They shrieked and jumped up and down in excitement as if they had been apart for months. They were eighth graders. This was going to be the best year yet. They each felt something more grown-up and exciting about the first day of eighth grade, and they were ready for it.

With a few minutes to spare before the bell rang, the girls stopped and leaned against their tree for a quick survey of the school yard. It was easy to identify the sixth graders. They were nervous, furtively glancing in every direction—the most telltale sign of a sixth grader—and had new outfits and two-day-old haircuts. The girls easily but not fondly remembered how scary it was to be new to middle school and felt sorry for the new sixth graders.

The seventh graders were a little more confident but still not nearly cool enough to speak to the eighth graders. Most students, no matter their grade, carried backpacks, and some had musical instruments. Some even had new glasses or had discarded their glasses in favor of contacts.

"Look over there." Kelly pointed across the grassy lawn to a student. A new student, obviously a sixth grader, struggled with his backpack and what appeared to be a saxophone case. Two bigger boys, eighth graders, grabbed the case out of his hands and held it over his head. They teased him mercilessly until the bell rang, forcing them to abandon their fun and head into the school. The girls shook their heads and sighed—some things never changed—as they began to walk toward the doors.

Kelly and Sam both stopped to reach into

their backpacks to turn off their new cell phones before entering the school—it would make for a horrible first day of school if they were to get their phones taken away.

"You're so lucky," Macy whined as she watched Kelly flip open her shiny blue phone, which was carefully decorated with sparkly gems. Sam laughed and turned off her sporty red phone, slid the top closed, and dropped it into her bag. Macy's parents wouldn't let her have a cell phone until high school.

"When did you guys get cell phones?" Lindsay asked.

"I got mine yesterday, and Sam got hers on Saturday," Kelly explained. "My mom wanted to have a way to reach me in case of an emergency and for me to be able to reach her. I'm not supposed to use it just anytime I want to."

"Same with me. I might as well not have it. I can call anyone who has the same service or use it as much as I want to on nights and weekends, but that's it," Sam complained.

"It's still way more than I have. You're so lucky," Macy whined.

Lindsay sighed while she smeared untinted

lip gloss onto her lips. "I have no idea when I'll ever get to have a cell phone. My mom thinks that they are bad for 'kids.' " She rolled her eyes to accentuate the point that she not only thought she should have a cell phone but that she definitely disagreed with the labeling of herself and her friends as *kids*. "She won't even let me use colored lip gloss. She thinks I'm too young."

With their cell phones turned off, backpacks slung over their shoulders, lip gloss perfectly accenting their skin tanned by the lazy days of summer, and their arms locked, the four best friends were ready to enter the school to begin their eighth-grade year.

Seeing their reflection in the glass doors of the school as they approached it, Lindsay noticed how tall they'd all become over the summer. Four pairs of new jeans, four similar T-shirts, and four long manes of shiny hair—they were similar in so many ways but different enough to keep things interesting.

Kelly Garrett was the leader of the group. The girls almost always looked to her to get the final word on anything from plans they might make, to boys they liked, to clothes they wore.

She was a natural leader, which was great most of the time. Her strong opinions sometimes caused conflict, though. Sam Lowell, the comedienne of the group, searched for ways to entertain them and make them laugh. She was willing to try anything once, and her friends enjoyed testing her on that. Macy Monroe was the sweet one. She was soft-spoken and slow to speak. She hated to offend anyone and got her feelings hurt easily. Then there was Lindsay. She was in the middle, the glue. She was strong but kind and was known to be a peacemaker.

Amid complete chaos—students talking, locker doors slamming shut, high fives, and whistles—the first day of school began. There was an assembly for the eighth graders, so the four girls headed toward the gymnasium together rather than finding their separate ways to their first classes.

The girls filed into the bleachers together, tucking their belongings carefully beneath their feet so nothing would fall through to the floor below. The room was raucously loud as 150 eighth graders excitedly shared stories of their summers and reunited with friends.

The speakers squealed as the principal turned on his microphone and tried to get everyone's attention. "Welcome back to Central Middle School. Let's all stand together to recite the Pledge of Allegiance."

Conversations slowly trailed off to a dull roar as teachers attempted to create some order in each row. The eighth graders shuffled to their feet and placed their right hands over their hearts to recite the pledge. The principal began: "I pledge allegiance to the flag. . . ."

Lindsay joined in, but her mind wandered as she looked down the row at each of her best friends. She thought back over the great summer they had just enjoyed. Together, they had spent many days languishing in the hot sun by Kelly's pool. She remembered the day when Sam got a bad sunburn from lying on the tanning raft for hours and not listening to the girls when they suggested that she reapply her sunscreen. She had wanted a good tan, and she paid the price. Kelly had the bright idea of using olive oil and lemon juice to take away the sting—she thought she'd heard that somewhere—but all it did was make Sam smell bad for days, along with the suffering that her burns caused.

They had gone shopping at the mall whenever Sam's mom would pile them into her SUV and drop them off for a few hours so they could check out the latest fashions and watch for new students—boys in particular. Their favorite mall activity was to take a huge order of cheese fries and four Diet Cokes to a table at the edge of the food court so they could watch the people walk by.

They had a blast burying each other in the sand at the beach whenever Macy's dad took a break from job hunting to spend the day lying in the sun. One time they even made a huge castle with a moat. The castle had steps they could climb, and the moat actually held water. It took them almost the entire day, but the pictures they took made it all worthwhile.

They had also shared a weeklong trip to Lindsay's Bible camp. It was a spiritual experience for Lindsay, who used the time to deepen her relationship with God. She enjoyed being able to bring her friends into that part of her life—even if it was just for a week. Macy, more than the others, showed some interest and said that she'd like to attend youth group with Lindsay when it started up again in the fall. All four girls enjoyed the canoe trips—even the one when the boat capsized and they got drenched. They swam in the lake and played beach volleyball. The week they spent at camp was a good end to what they considered a perfect summer.

Although there was a certain finality to their fun and freedom with the arrival of the school year, it offered excitement, too, as they took this next step toward growing up together. What would it be like in the future? In just one year they would start high school together. After several years, they would head off to the same college and room together, as the plan had always been. At some point, they would each find someone to settle down with and get married. They had already figured out who would be the maid of honor for whose wedding. That way they each got to do it once. And they would be bridesmaids for each other. Then they would have children. Hopefully they would have them at around the same time so their children could grow up together, too. Beautiful plans built on beautiful friendships. . . what more could a girl ask for?

". . .One nation, under God, indivisible, with liberty and justice for all." The Pledge of Allegiance ended, and all the students sat down to hear about the exciting new school year.

Chapter 2

THIS IS REAL WORK

Second period—the dreaded class two periods before lunch—seemed to drag on forever with lunch still two hours away and the day stretching on so long ahead of it. But not for Lindsay, Kelly, Macy, and Sam; they loved second period this year. Not only was it their favorite class—home economics—but it was also the only class that they all had together. It was like a little break in the day.

On the first day of school, Mrs. Portney, the much-loved home ec teacher, allowed them to break into groups of four. It would be in those groups that the class would work on cooking, sewing, and other craft projects. Of course, the Lindsay-Kelly-Macy-Sam group was a no brainer, and the girls quickly arranged their seating so they could be together.

The first project for the class was to make a stuffed pillow—but not just any stuffed pillow. This one had to be special, unique, and creative. They were allowed to use felt, stuffing, and any other craft materials they wanted. Things like pipe cleaners, movable eyes, glitter, rhinestones, fabric markers, and stencils were all available to the class. Or they could bring things from home to contribute to their project. They had ten minutes to put their heads together to decide what to make.

"What about a teddy bear pillow?" Lindsay suggested.

"No, someone makes that every year," Kelly said, shaking her head. "We want to do something really interesting."

"Hmm. How about a rainbow pillow?" Lindsay tried again.

"Nah, too boring," Sam replied.

"Oh! We could make a bicycle pillow with real wheels that spin." Macy suggested.

The girls laughed. "Who would want to lay on that?"

"We could do a big heart that says 'Macy loves Tyler' and put an arrow through it," Kelly teased.

"Yeah, right." Macy laughed.

"I know!" Sam said, getting excited. "Why don't we do a Mrs. Portney pillow?"

The other girls just looked at her for a minute, not quite sure if she was serious or if she had lost her mind—or both.

"Well, we could make it really fluffy, just like Mrs. Portney. We'll put an apron on the pillow, just like the one Mrs. Portney wears. We'll give the pillow a cute pair of round glasses made out of felt and use a shiny fabric as the glass part."

"Yeah," Kelly jumped in, liking the idea and adding some suggestions. "We can put scissors, pencils, and a tape measure hanging out of her apron pocket."

"We'll put her in a navy blue dress just like the one that Mrs. Portney wears all the time," Macy added.

"And then," Lindsay jumped on board, "we'll make it a gift to Mrs. Portney when we're done."

All four girls agreed that it was a winning idea, and they just couldn't wait to get started. They looked around the room and saw that the other groups were struggling over ideas and having a difficult time getting started.

"Class, when you have your ideas, please just write them down on a slip of paper, along with the names of the students who are in your group, and turn it in to me before class is over today."

"Uh, Mrs. Portney?" Sam hesitantly raised her hand.

"Yes, what is it, Samantha?" Mrs. Portney asked. She was the only teacher who didn't annoy Sam when she called her by her full name.

"Well, we were just wondering. . . ." Sam spoke for the group. "Can we keep our pillow idea a secret until we're done? It's kind of a surprise."

"Oh?" Mrs. Portney grinned at the possibilities and shifted her glasses down to peer at the four girls over the top of them. "I suppose that would be all right, even though it's highly unusual. But then again, what else should I expect from you four? As long as you understand that if you don't tell me what you're doing, I can't help guide you in the process. But even without my help, you're still responsible for every part of the project in order to get a full grade."

"No problem, Mrs. Portney. Thanks!"

The bell rang, and it was time to head off to their separate classes. Kelly had English, Macy had math, Lindsay went to social studies, and Sam headed off to PE.

"Ugh! What happened to summer?" Kelly lamented to her friends as they slumped toward the cafeteria for lunch on Wednesday during the second week of school.

"I know exactly what you mean," Lindsay replied. "I thought they had to give you a few weeks before they started piling on the homework, but I think I already have two hours of homework for tonight, and the day is only half over."

"So much for eighth grade being so great," Sam laughingly agreed as she collapsed in her seat with her lunch tray.

"What's with you?" Lindsay asked Macy when she noticed that Macy had hardly said a word since they met up by their lockers a few minutes before.

"Oh, nothing really," Macy moped. Her friends just looked at her, waiting, not about to let her off the hook that easily. "Well, it's just that my math class is much harder this year, and I barely made it through last year's class. My mom has been talking about a tutor, and I don't want to have to do that." She slumped her shoulders and dropped her head onto her arms after pushing away her lunch tray.

"Can we help?" Lindsay offered. "We could help you study. I have the same class as you, and Kelly is ahead of both of us."

"Yeah," Kelly jumped in. "If all of us help, you should be able to pull out of this, no problem."

"I don't know." Macy wasn't convinced. "I already failed my first quiz. I just don't have a math brain, I guess. I think I'm prepared, but then the test starts, and I can't remember any-thing about the formulas and the order of the steps. You can help me study, but I think my memory is the problem. . .or something like that." Macy looked defeated.

Sam jumped up with an idea. "I know!" she shouted.

Lindsay and Kelly were startled by her outburst and almost knocked over their drinks.

"What's gotten into you, silly?" Kelly asked, laughing.

"Well," Sam continued, "Saturday is only

three days away. Let's have a sleepover at my house. We'll celebrate making it through the second week of school by eating some junk food, watching some movies, and staying up late. What do you say?"

"Oh, count me in!" Kelly jumped at the chance.

"Me, too!" Macy quickly added.

"Well, you guys know my mom won't let me stay out on a Saturday because of church on Sunday, so you'll have to count me out," Lindsay replied.

"Oh no!" Sam shook her head. She held up a finger so she could finish chewing her bite of food, swallowed, grabbed a quick drink of milk to wash it down, and said, "No way are we leaving you out. We'll do it Friday." To a chorus of agreement from the other girls, Lindsay agreed to the plans, and the girls were relieved to have something fun to look forward to.

"Now let's make a list," Macy, ever the planner, suggested, excited to be able to move on from the depressing talk of her math class. "What should we do, and what should we bring?"

"Definitely a movie," Kelly suggested.

"Okay. And we can't do a movie without a pizza." Macy wrote MOVIE and PIZZA on the list.

"What about a game?" Lindsay asked.

"Oh, girls, I have a game for us, but it's a surprise. You'll have to wait until Friday night to find out what it is," Sam teased.

"Sounds mysterious." Macy wrote down: SAM'S SECRET GAME. And all of the girls giggled. They made their plans for Friday night and agreed that it would be a nice diversion to what was shaping up to be a tough year.

Macy, who was watching her weight as usual, picked the sausage and pepperoni off her pizza. Kelly, who never worried about her weight, silently reached over to grab Macy's pepperoni.

"Hey!" Macy smacked her hand away. "What are you doing?"

"Well, you're not going to eat them."

"No, but I'd rather not have it shoved in my face that you can eat anything you want and never gain weight!" Macy whined.

"My mom gets so mad when I talk about dieting or watching what I'm eating," Lindsay said. "She thinks we're too young to worry about it and that we should just enjoy being kids."

"No one wants to get fat," Kelly snorted. "And we aren't kids, but we aren't grown-ups yet either, so I'm not going to worry about it just yet."

"I agree that no one wants to be fat," Lindsay countered, "but we should be careful and think about what we eat because it's healthier, not so we can be skinny."

"Easy for you to say," Macy grumbled.

"I'm not skinny at all," Lindsay said defensively.

"No, not skinny, but you're not fat either. You're perfect."

"Oh, I don't feel perfect. I don't think anyone does," Lindsay explained. "I just think we should be able to relax about things a little more. There's too much pressure to be what other people want us to be. As long as we're happy about who we are inside, that should be enough for people to be friends with us, right?"

"It's not like it's something you have to choose between, Linds. I mean, we can be nice and skinny at the same time, right?" Sam was confused.

"Of course you can. I'm just talking about priorities. I don't want to be the kind of person who looks at someone's outside appearance and judges them on whether they're skinny enough or not."

"True," Sam agreed. "But unfortunately, not everyone feels that way. And for that reason, I'll stick to my salad and skip the french fries when we go out to eat."

"Yeah, and if you don't mind," Macy replied, still irritated, "I'll pick off my pepperoni if I want to."

"Okay, okay, okay." Lindsay gave in, laughing. "I was just trying to give us a new outlook. You guys are perfect in my book, no matter how you look."

Chapter 3

SLEEPOVER PARTY

"Mom, did you hear the doorbell ring?" Sam shouted excitedly, forgetting that her mom wasn't even home. She'd been waiting for her friends for what seemed like hours. Running to the front door, Sam swung it wide open to find Kelly and Macy. The three girls squealed in excitement, and Kelly turned to wave at her mom as she backed out of the driveway with a little honk. They all turned to look down the street, anxious because they couldn't get started without Lindsay. With Lindsay nowhere in sight, they dropped to the porch step to wait until she arrived.

"She's here! She's here!" the girls yelled when Lindsay's mom pulled into the driveway to drop her off for the night.

"Hi, Mrs. Martin." Sam waved a greeting.

Mrs. Martin chuckled at the girls' excitement. "You girls see each other almost every single day. How can you get so excited over just one more day?"

"Oh, Mrs. Martin, this is different," Sam assured her. "This is a special night. It's our first sleepover as eighth graders."

"Well, all right." Mrs. Martin laughed and rolled her eyes. "Just be sure that you eighth graders stay out of trouble."

"We will," the girls promised.

"Now come on!" Sam linked arms with Kelly, Kelly grabbed Lindsay's arm, Lindsay grabbed Macy, and they all started to walk in together.

Mrs. Martin honked and waved. Through her open window, she reminded Lindsay, "You remember what I said—be good."

The girls walked together into the house, squealing and giggling all the way.

"What should we do first?" Kelly asked.

"My mom bought all the stuff for us to make pizza, and she left instructions for us. She and Dad went to a friend's house for dinner and won't be home until later, so she thought that would be fun for us," Sam explained.

"Cool!" The girls agreed it would be fun to make their own pizza, and knowing how long things could take when they started messing around, they got started right away.

Looking at the list, Sam got out the ingredients. There was dough to unroll, sauce to spread, cheese to sprinkle, and, of course, pepperoni to put on top.

"Oops. . .we almost forgot. It says to preheat the oven to four hundred degrees," Sam told the girls.

"I'll get that," Lindsay said, since she was standing right in front of the oven. Sam dug out pizza pans, and the other girls washed their hands and rolled up their sleeves.

Pizza Instructions
1. *Preheat the oven to 400 degrees.*
2. *Spray the pizza pan with nonstick spray, and sprinkle with flour.*
3. *Spread the dough onto the pizza pan evenly.*
4. *Evenly apply the pizza sauce to cover the dough.*
5. *Sprinkle the cheese all over the pizza.*

6. *Spread the pepperoni on the top of the pizza.*
7. *Bake for approximately 15–18 minutes, checking it regularly.*
8. *Be careful when you take it out. It's going to be HOT!*

Lindsay said, "I'll do the spray."

"I'll sprinkle the flour," said Kelly. When it came time for that, she got a mischievous look on her face and flicked her fingers at Lindsay and Sam, who were standing nearby.

"Hey!" The girls giggled as they shook their long hair over the sink to get the flour out.

Sam spread the sauce, and they all took turns sprinkling the cheese. They worked on spreading the pepperoni until the pizza was completely covered and then added a few more just to make sure. Into the oven it went.

Sam set the timer, and the girls turned to take a look at the kitchen that they needed to clean while the pizza cooked. What a disaster! With a chorus of four loud groans, they started cleaning up their mess, wishing they hadn't been so sloppy while they prepared the pizza. They had to put all the ingredients away, clean up the dishes, wipe off the countertops, and clean the floor. Eventually, though, they had the kitchen restored to what they thought was its original condition. Sam's mom might disagree, but hopefully it would be good enough.

Sam's mom had picked up some movies for them from the rental store, they chose one to watch on Sam's huge plasma television screen while they ate their pizza, which had finished baking at almost the exact time that they finished their cleaning. Armed with plates piled high with pizza and cans of soda, they settled in on the big leather sofa in the basement to watch their movie.

After a little while, Sam nudged Lindsay. "Hey, look over there." Sam pointed to Kelly, who was sound asleep on the sofa. The girls giggled quietly.

"Hmm...what should we do to her?" Lindsay asked the girls—because, as everyone knew, the first person to fall asleep at a sleepover got pranked. It was usually Macy who fell asleep first, but now it was Kelly's turn.

"We could fill her shoes with shaving cream," Sam suggested. The girls laughed but dismissed the idea because Kelly wouldn't discover it until the next morning, which would be no fun—plus they could get in trouble if her shoes got ruined. So, after conspiring together for a few minutes, they concocted a pretty devious plan that they were quite proud of.

Sam went to the kitchen to fill a glass with very cold water and even added a few ice cubes to it to make sure it was cold enough. They balanced the glass very carefully on the back frame of the couch, which was leaning against the wall, and then propped it there with the little decorative pillows that Sam's mom had sitting around on the sofa. They made sure that the only direction the glass could fall was forward. The three girls tiptoed to the door and quietly left the room. When they made it out the door, Sam reached back, took the doorknob, and pulled really hard.

Bam! The door slammed shut. The girls quickly opened the door just a crack so they could see the scene they had created.

With the slamming of the door, Kelly immediately woke up and looked around the room, half asleep and confused. Startled and seeing that she was alone, she sat up abruptly. The pillows supporting the water glass were disturbed, and the glass tumbled forward, drenching Kelly from her neck all the way down the front of her shirt with ice-cold water.

She squealed as the water touched her skin and her body shivered. Her eyes flashed in anger as she searched for someone. . .anyone. Then she heard the girls trying really hard not to giggle, and even though she tried not to laugh, she couldn't help herself. When the other three saw that she was being a good sport, they tumbled through the door, laughing so hard they could barely stand up straight. Sam fell to the tiled basement floor in fits of laughter as Kelly grabbed a towel from the laundry pile to dry herself.

"It serves. . .you right. . .for falling asleep . . .so early!" Lindsay tried to talk in between gales of laughter.

"Okay, okay, I get it." Kelly gave in, shaking her head. "But you had all better be careful, because I am well rested now, and I'll be up long after all of you fall asleep." The girls laughed good-naturedly.

They carried their dishes and garbage upstairs to the kitchen so they could make sure everything was cleaned up before Sam's mom and dad got home.

"So, Macy. . . ," Kelly hesitantly began while they were straightening the kitchen.

"Yeah?" Macy raised a skeptical eyebrow.

"What's the deal with you and Tyler Turner this year?"

Lindsay and Sam stopped what they were doing. Sam turned off the water in the sink so she could hear Macy's reply.

"What are you talking about?" Macy asked innocently but smiled as she looked away.

"Oh no! Don't even think about pretending that you don't know what I'm talking about." Kelly wagged her finger.

"She's blushing!" Lindsay shouted when Macy's cheeks turned bright red.

"No, I'm not blushing," Macy insisted. "I'm just hot."

"Right! Sure!" The girls didn't believe her and continued demanding answers. "It's time to fess up," Lindsay insisted.

"All right, all right," Macy relented. "The thing is, I don't know what is going on with Tyler. I mean, you guys know that I've liked him forever—like, for two whole years. But I don't think he knows that I exist. But then sometimes it feels like he likes me, too."

"Right—I mean, how do you explain the fact that every time I leave my science class, he's there by your locker, waiting for you to come out of math? Hmm?" Kelly pried.

"He's just being nice," Macy insisted. She continued. "What do you think I should do? I mean, my parents probably wouldn't let me date anyway, so I guess it's all for the best."

"Here's what we'll do." Sam jumped in with an idea. "I'll ask his cousin Stephanie, whose brother, Kenny, is Tyler's best friend, if he likes you. But I won't tell her who wants to know."

Kelly and Lindsay loved the idea, but Macy was hesitant. "Oh, I don't know. . . ."

"Oh, you should totally do that. It's perfect," Kelly insisted.

"Okay," Macy agreed. "As long as he doesn't find out that you asked for me."

"Deal!" Sam assured her, and the girls high-fived each other.

They heard the garage door start to open. With a little squeal, they hurriedly put away the last item and rushed out of the kitchen, turning off the lights on their way out. Trying to avoid the parents, the girls rushed downstairs to the basement, where they planned to sleep all night. Sam's mom popped her head downstairs for a quick second just to let the girls know they were home and then headed upstairs to bed.

As soon as they heard the bedroom door close upstairs, Sam got a glimmer in her eye and began to look at the girls, one at a time, teasing them until they remembered.

"Oh!" Macy exclaimed, catching on. "Let's play Sam's secret game."

"We can do that. But only if you're sure you're ready. . . ," Sam teased mysteriously. "There are some rules."

"We're ready," everyone agreed a bit hesi-tantly, wondering what Sam had cooked up for them this time.

Chapter 4

TRUTH OR DARE

"So?" Lindsay started. "Let's have it, Sam. What is this game you've kept such a secret all week?"

"Yeah, let's play," the other two girls chimed in.

"Well, if you're sure you want to play," Sam explained, "you have to really agree to play for real, no matter what. It's a matter of honor."

"How can we agree if we don't know what the game is?" Lindsay asked nervously.

"Well, all I can tell you until you agree is that the game is called Truth or Dare, and the key to it is that there are no limits. And you can't bail out."

"How do you play?" Kelly asked.

"Yeah," Macy prodded. "You have to tell us the rules before we can agree to it."

"Me, too. No way am I agreeing without knowing what I'm agreeing to." Lindsay folded her arms.

"Well, basically it's like this: When it's your turn, you choose whether you want a truth or a dare," Sam explained. "If you choose Truth, you will be asked a question that you have to answer truthfully. You cannot back out if you don't like the question. If you choose Dare, then you will be given a task—or a dare—that you must complete. You can't just decide that it's too hard or too risky. You *have* to do it. If you're scared that you won't be able to follow through, then you shouldn't agree to play at all."

"You mean we can't set any limits ahead of time, like about things we aren't allowed to do?" Lindsay was pretty nervous about the rules of the game.

"Nope. If you're too scared about what your dare might be, then just choose Truth. What have you got to hide, anyway?" Sam laughed as she sat down on the carpet. She knew that Lindsay had no deep, dark secrets.

"I'm in!" Kelly shouted, joining Sam on the floor.

"Count me in," Macy added, joining them to make a half circle, leaving room for Lindsay.

"Well, I guess I'll play." Lindsay shrugged. Couldn't hurt.

"Great! Then I'll go first. I'll choose Truth to get us started," Sam said.

The other three girls went into the corner to whisper for a few minutes about what to ask Sam, who was waiting on the floor. Giggling, they returned to the circle and took their places. Since Lindsay was seated right next to Sam and it would be her turn next, she asked the question: "Sam, have you ever taken something that didn't belong to you? And we mean, since you've been older than, say, fifth grade," Lindsay clarified.

"Ooh, good question." Sam was impressed that the game had gotten off to a great start. After contemplating her answer, she replied, "Yeah, this one time in sixth grade, I really, really wanted this pack of stickers from the card store, and I decided to take them when my mom wasn't looking. When we got back into the car, she noticed them and made me return them. I got into a *lot* of trouble for that."

Laughing at Sam's story, the girls turned their

attention to Lindsay who had to select a truth or a dare for her turn. Lindsay, becoming slightly more confident in the game, selected Truth, too. The three girls left Lindsay sitting on the floor while they discussed what they should ask her as her Truth question. It seemed to take a long time, and Lindsay began to impatiently pick at her nails while she waited for them. Finally they scurried back to the floor and resumed their spots in the circle.

Kelly, who was sitting next to Lindsay, got to ask the next Truth question. "Lindsay, your Truth question is: Do you ever hate going to church or resent that your parents make you go all the time?"

Lindsay hesitated over that one. She knew she had to tell the truth, but she also wanted to protect her witness and make sure she wasn't misrepresenting her feelings about God, her church, and her parents. . .but she had to tell the truth. "Well, it's not that I ever 'hate' going to church; I love my church. And I don't 'resent' my parents for making me go all the time. I know they just want what's best for me. But sometimes it's a drag to have to miss out on fun things and

TRUTH OR DARE

not be able to make plans several times a week because of church activities. Overall, though, I don't think I would trade it." Satisfied with her answer, she breathed a deep sigh of relief and felt that her honesty probably did more good for her cause than hurt it.

Kelly's turn. "I pick Dare!"

"How did I guess?" Macy laughed. The girls eagerly got up from the floor, letting Kelly wait there patiently while they decided what she was to do for her dare. There were lots of whispers and giggles coming from the other side of the room, which made Kelly squirm nervously, a bit afraid of what she'd gotten herself into. After waiting for about five minutes, she called over to the girls, "Come on now, this is the first dare. Go easy."

After a few more minutes, the girls came rushing back to the floor and resumed a lopsided, halfhearted circle. Macy couldn't wait to tell Kelly what her dare was. She informed Kelly that she had to sneak upstairs into Sam's brother's room and take his baseball cleats while he was sleeping in the room and then soak them in water and put them in the freezer!

45

"Oh man! You girls are rotten." Kelly laughed but immediately rose to begin her dare.

She crept up the stairs with the other girls following her and paused in front of the closed bedroom door. Kelly took a deep breath and then slowly pushed it open. They could see the rise and fall of the covers on the bed as Sam's brother breathed deeply in his sleep. Kelly carefully opened the door a little more so she could get into the room without making a noise. It squeaked a little bit when she pushed on it, but Sam's brother didn't wake up or even stir.

Kelly made her way across the room, stepping over a soccer ball, two pair of shoes, a couple of piles of clothes, and some magazines. When she got near the bed, she looked around the room and finally spotted the baseball cleats. They were hanging on a peg right above the headboard of the bed on the opposite side.

She looked back at the girls in the doorway, who were trying really hard not to laugh out loud. Nearing the bed, she tried to hold her breath so she would make less noise. Slowly she leaned across the bed, being very careful not to touch it or slip and fall onto it. The thought of that paralyzed her for a moment as she imagined falling on top of Sam's brother and him waking up. Shaking her head to clear the thought, she knew that no matter what she couldn't let that happen. So she firmly planted her feet and reached across the bed toward the cleats hanging on the wall across from her.

She couldn't reach them!

Hearing muffled giggles from the hallway, she shot an angry look at the girls, telling them to be quiet. Kelly backed up a little bit and looked for something she could use to unhook the shoes from their peg.

Aha! She spotted a pair of crutches that Sam's brother had to use when he hurt his ankle a few months ago. She silently lifted one of the crutches and pointed it toward the baseball cleats. She leaned carefully until the bottom of the crutch was hooked into the tied-together laces of the cleats. She slowly lifted the crutch and freed the cleats from their perch on the peg, turning carefully so that the cleats were no longer hanging over the bed. Bending slowly to the floor, Kelly laid everything down onto the floor and then stepped over to grab the cleats and put the crutch back where she found it.

After creeping out of the room and closing the door behind her, the girls all ran to the kitchen and collapsed into fits of laughter. Kelly was out of breath, and her hands were shaking.

But her dare wasn't quite over, the other girls reminded her.

Looking in the kitchen cabinets, Kelly found an old pot that she filled with water. After hesitating for just a moment, she dropped the shoes into the water. Sam cleared a place in the freezer, and Kelly put in the pot. Then they scurried back down to the basement where they laughed so hard they had to wipe tears from their eyes. "Boy, I sure hope he doesn't have a baseball game tomorrow," Kelly said.

"It's not baseball season, anyway," Macy reminded them. "I just hope he finds them before Sam's mom does."

The thought of Sam's mom opening the freezer in the morning to find a pot of shoes inside started the giggles all over again.

Macy's turn.

"Oh man, I'm scared to pick Dare," Macy admitted.

"Go for it. We've had two Truths already," the

other girls encouraged her.

"Okay, let's get it over with," Macy giggled. "I pick Dare."

The three girls rushed over to the corner to discuss what the dare should be. Almost immediately, Sam rushed over to the desk in the corner and grabbed the phone book. They tore through it until they found what they're looking for. Scribbling furiously on a piece of paper, they start to giggle.

Macy's face looked stricken with dread.

When they got back to the circle, Kelly thrust a scrap of paper at Macy. Macy was confused when she saw that a phone number had been hastily scribbled on the paper. "Whose number is this, and what am I supposed to do with it?"

Kelly explained, "You need to call that number, and when the machine picks up, say, 'This is Macy Monroe. Can you come out to play?' And then hang up."

"That sounds simple enough, but whose number is it, and what if they answer?"

"Mace, we're not going to tell you whose number it is—that's part of the dare. And if they answer, you still have to say it. But they probably won't answer. It's almost two in the morning."

"Okay, let's just do this." Macy couldn't wait to get it over with, so she immediately began to dial the phone. Sam reached over to put the phone on speaker so they all could hear. It rang three times and then a fourth time, when the answering machine finally picked up.

"Hello, you've reached the Turner residence." Macy's eyes got really wide; she gasped and started to panic. ". . .No one is available to answer your call right now. . .please leave a message after the beep."

"Um. . .hello. . .this is Macy. . . . Um. . .can you. . .um. . .come out to play?" And then she hung up, embarrassed and red faced. The other three girls were laughing uncontrollably and rolling on the floor.

Macy, trying to be a good sport by pretending it was no big deal, shrugged and said, "Okay, now what?" The other three knew she was bluffing, and that made them laugh even harder.

"What? It's no big deal. I don't care."

"Riiiight, like it doesn't bother you at all. You got sick to your stomach, and we all know it," Kelly teased.

"Well, how would you like to embarrass yourself like that? It wasn't fun, that's for sure."

"It was kind of fun for us." Sam laughed, and the others agreed.

"So, judging by the yawns that have been going around the circle, I'd say it's time to get some sleep. What do you think?" Sam asked the group.

They'd had way more than enough fun for one night but agreed they would definitely play Truth or Dare again. They got out their toothbrushes and blankets and got ready for bed. Once settled, it still took them over an hour to actually stop chatting and fall asleep, but eventually they all dozed off with smiles on their faces.

Chapter 5

SUNDAY SCHOOL

"Rise and shine!" Lindsay's mom called from the doorway, letting her know it was time to get up and get ready for church.

"Ugh. Mom, can I just sleep in this one time? Please?" Lindsay groaned. "I promise I'll go next week."

"Oh no. You know better than that, young lady. We always go to church as a family, and this week will be no different."

Lindsay pulled the covers over her head and stopped short of saying something to her mom that she might live to regret.

"Breakfast is in fifteen minutes," Lindsay's mom said as she left the room.

She knew that there was no way out of it. She

also knew that if she let her mom know just how tired she was, Lindsay wouldn't be allowed to do sleepovers with the girls anymore, especially if it interfered with church. She slowly sat up and let her eyes grow accustomed to the bright sunshine that filled her room. Sleepily she made her way to the bathroom in the hallway, where she brushed her teeth and her hair—grateful that she had taken a shower the night before—and splashed water on her face. Lindsay applied just the barest hint of makeup, hoping it would help liven her face and keep her from looking so tired.

Shuffling back to her bedroom, she pulled open her closet door and began to sort through her dresses and skirts, looking for an outfit that would perk her up. Finding just the perfect thing, Lindsay slipped into a light brown skirt cut just above the knee—almost too short for her mom's taste—and a cute denim top. On her way out of the room, she stopped in front of the mirror and clipped her hair back on one side with a silver butterfly clip, sprayed on a squirt of perfume, and, satisfied with the finished product, headed downstairs with two minutes to spare.

"Well, there she is," Mom said in her usually cheery voice.

"I was thinking we'd have to send in the troops to drag her out," Lindsay's dad added.

Rolling her eyes and laughing, Lindsay reached for her plate and took a spoonful of scrambled eggs and two pieces of bacon.

"Father," her dad began to pray, "please bless this food and nourish our bodies and our souls today. We give this day to You to use for Your glory. Amen." Lindsay and her mom added their amens and began to eat.

On the way to church, Lindsay's mom turned in her seat so that she could see Lindsay. "So, how was Friday night over at Sam's? What did you girls do all night?"

"Oh, it was fun. We stayed up kind of late and talked and played some games."

"What kind of games did you play?" Mrs. Martin pressed uncharacteristically.

"Oh, nothing really, just some different games and one that Sam made up." Lindsay wondered what her mom was getting at—this line of questioning seemed a little out of the ordinary.

"Well, I got a call from Mrs. Lowell, Sam's mom. It seems that she got up this morning and went to make some breakfast. She was surprised to find something in the freezer. What do you suppose she found there, Linds?"

"It was just a dare that Kelly had to do. She . . .um. . .well, you probably already know what she had to do," Lindsay stammered, trying not to laugh.

"Yes, it appears that she put Scott Lowell's baseball shoes in a pot of water and froze them," her mom said sternly.

Even from her spot in the backseat, Lindsay could see that her dad was trying very hard not to laugh—and he was losing the battle.

"Whatever possessed you girls to do that?" Mrs. Martin asked.

"Oh, come on," Lindsay's dad jumped in. "It's just a harmless prank. We all did things like that. It's a pretty clever one, too, if you ask me."

Relieved that she had her dad on her side, Lindsay looked back at her mom, who was carefully choosing her next words.

"Lindsay, I just want you to be aware that harmless pranks can still be costly to people and cause harm. Also, one harmless prank often leads to another until, before you know it, you're trapped into doing something that never would have happened if you hadn't gone down that road to begin with. Do you know what I'm saying, sweetie?"

"Yeah, Mom, I get it. I'll be careful. I promise."

"Just keep in mind what I said. Damage can be done even when you think it's perfectly harmless."

As soon as the car pulled into the church parking lot, Lindsay jumped out and ran ahead to join her youth group friends on the lawn, before another word could be said about the sleepover.

"Would you all please stand for the reading of God's Word?" Pastor Tim paused to wait for the congregation to rise to their feet. "Today's reading will be taken from the book of First Thessalonians, chapter 5." He read to them from the Bible, and then everyone sat down for the sermon.

In his sermon, Pastor Tim showed how the Bible warned Christians to avoid even the appearance of evil. "Think about what that means and why we would need a warning like that. I mean, sin is sin, right? Appearing to sin isn't the same thing as actually doing it, is it? So why would we be warned in scripture to avoid even looking like we are involved in evil things? I'll tell you why. It's because God asks us to be His ambassadors. He calls us to bring the light of His love to this dying world. How can we possibly do that if we are involved in things that appear to be evil or sinful? Whether we're guilty or not doesn't matter at that point. All that matters is that when a Christian seems to be doing wrong, he is assumed to be a hypocrite, and Christianity suffers. Satan just waits for Christians to make mistakes—or, in the case of what we're talking about today, to even appear to make mistakes. Then he can capitalize on those mistakes and use them against the cause of Christ.

"So take care not to find yourself in questionable situations. One way to do this is to really think and pray about the people you consider to be your friends. As my mother always told me, 'You are known by the company you keep.' That means that what your friends are known for, you will be known for, too. If your friends are known for questionable behavior, it will be assumed that you condone and participate in it.

"Also, we are all susceptible to the effects of temptation. Sin creeps in slowly and grabs hold of us before we even realize it. Your intentions can be completely pure, but over time the line between what is right and what is wrong becomes fuzzy. Eventually, if you allow yourself to be exposed to sinful behavior, it won't seem so bad and you'll forget your resolve, giving in to temptation and peer pressure. Think of it like a dark mist that slowly engulfs you. At first, you barely see the mist, but eventually you can barely see anything else because of it."

Pastor Tim's words made a lot of sense. Lindsay was grateful for her friends and that they were good girls. But being in eighth grade and knowing that high school was right around the corner, Lindsay promised herself it was advice that she would follow.

Pastor Tim closed the service, and everyone stood up to leave. On their way out, Lindsay's mom and dad stopped to talk to several friends. Knowing that it would take them a long time to make their way to the car, Lindsay went to see if she could find any of her youth group buddies. She headed over to the new addition to the church that was still under construction. Pulling back the plastic that hung as a divider between the current church and the new building, she stepped in among the dust and tools to see if anyone was hanging out in there. It had become the typical place for teens to go during the church service to hang out when they didn't want to actually sit through the service.

"Hey, you guys! What's up?" Lindsay asked the three teens she found back there.

Scott, Tanner, and Christy had seen someone coming and were scurrying to hide something. When they saw that it was Lindsay, they relaxed a little bit.

"What are you guys doing back here?" Lindsay asked.

"Oh, we're just hanging out, chatting, you know," Tanner answered.

"Okay, fine, don't tell me what's really going on." Lindsay laughed, knowing that there was more to the story.

"Lindsay, if you promise not to say anything, I'll show you." Christy pulled out a pack of cigarettes and a lighter from behind her back. "Want one?"

Thinking back to Pastor Tim's sermon, Lindsay realized that if someone happened upon them at just that moment, Lindsay would immediately appear just as guilty as the others. She hadn't smoked the cigarettes, and she didn't even think it was okay that the others had. But still, it would be assumed that she was involved in it or at least condoned the behavior just because she was hanging out with them. She knew that her best bet was to get out of there right away.

"Uh, no thanks. I really need to get going." Lindsay left immediately and went to find her parents, grateful she hadn't been forced to learn this lesson the hard way.

Lindsay could hear her computer chirping for her the instant they entered the house after having lunch with some of her parents' friends after church. She was getting instant messages, and lots of them. Rushing to her room, she saw her messenger program lit up like a Christmas tree. Sam, Kelly, and Macy were all online and trying to get her to show up for a chat session. Knowing that these chat sessions could take hours, Lindsay ran to get a can of soda before she settled in and let them know she was there.

"Linds," her mom called, hearing her in the kitchen, "if you're planning to get on the computer, you only have about thirty minutes before we head over to your grandma's—don't forget."

"No problem, Mom," Lindsay replied, not letting her mom know that she had, in fact, forgotten about the visit.

Rushing back to her room, Lindsay plopped down into her chair and typed a message to the group. *I'm here!*

Macy: *Hi, stranger!*

Kelly: *Where've u been?*

Lindsay: *Church, just got home, and I have to leave in 30. So what's up?*

Sam: *Kelly has a plan. She's just getting ready to tell us.*

Lindsay: *Cool! What is it?*

Kelly: *The other night was a blast, right?*

Lindsay: *Oh yeah!*

Macy: *Total blast!*

Sam: *Definitely!*

Kelly: *So let's make it a tradition. Let's have a sleepover every Friday at a different house.*

Macy: *I'm in!*

Sam: *Me, too, probably. I'll have to ask my mom; she's still kind of mad about the shoes. I guess my brother thinks he should get new shoes out of the deal.*

Macy: *lol*

Kelly: *LOL! Just give her some time. She'll be ready by the time it's your turn again. What do you say, Linds?*

Lindsay: *Oh sure, count me in!*

Sam: *So whose house is next, then?*

Macy: *I'll go next. My dad's going to be out of town this weekend, so my mom won't mind having us there.*

Lindsay: *Sounds good to me.*

Kelly: *Okay, then I'll go next.*

Sam: *Great!*

Lindsay: *After Kelly is my turn.*

Kelly: *Perfect! And we can play our game every time. It will be our tradition.*

Lindsay: *Didn't we cause enough trouble last time?*

Macy: *Yeah! I still can't look Tyler Turner in the eye!*

Sam: *And my mom was really mad about the shoes.*

Kelly: *That's part of the game. It's a risk. That's what makes it fun. We can make a rule that nothing we do can be destructive to anyone's property. How about that?*

Lindsay: *I think that def. should be the rule!*

Sam: *I agree.*

Macy: *Definitely!*

Lindsay: *Sounds like a plan. I have to run!*

Macy: *C U later!*

Kelly: *C U guys tomorrow!*

Sam: *Bye!*

After signing off her instant messenger program, Lindsay paused for a moment and considered the message of Pastor Tim's sermon this morning: Sin is slow; it creeps in like a dark mist, and you don't realize it until it engulfs you and everything around you until you can't see anything clearly. *I hope that doesn't ever happen to me.* But why worry? Everything was great. There was nothing to be concerned about.

Chapter 6

HOSTESS MACY

"What time should we be at your house tonight, Macy?" Lindsay asked, referring to the sleepover party they had planned for that night.

"Oh, anytime after five would be fine, I think. My dad is leaving for his trip this morning, and Mom likes to be home when I have friends over, as you all already know," Macy replied, rolling her eyes.

"Yeah, my parents are like that, too," Lindsay replied just as the bell rang, which signified that class was about to begin.

"Good morning, boys and girls," Mrs. Portney began the class. "Go ahead and get your projects out of your bins." One student from each group shuffled toward the bank of yellow bins in the cupboards on the wall where they had stored their project materials, notes, and scraps between classes. The bin for each group was clearly labeled with the names of each group and what they had chosen to make—except for Lindsay, Kelly, Sam, and Macy's bin. On theirs, it only said their names because of the special permission to keep their project a secret until it was finished.

The big yellow bins were placed on the tables in front of the group members, and the students awaited further instructions.

"Class," Mrs. Portney said, "I'd like for you to take a moment to make notes in your project notebook of what supplies and materials you've used and exactly how much you think you will use to complete the project. Then estimate the total cost of materials for your project. You can designate a group secretary for note-taking and then go ahead and get started. There is a supply list in the notebook on the front table if you need to consult it for names and prices of goods that have been provided to you. If there is something you have brought from home and you don't know the price, make an estimate and then write a question mark next to it so that we will know later on that it was only an estimate."

The girls took a look inside their bin and removed their materials from the brown paper bags. They spread out the piles of felt that they intended to use to make the body and the clothes, the aluminum foil for the eyeglasses, the movable eyes they would affix to Mrs. Portney's face, and all of the other supplies that they had contributed but weren't yet sure they would use.

"Mrs. Portney?" Lindsay raised her hand.

"Yes, Ms. Martin," Mrs. Portney responded.

"What about the things that we have in our bins that we aren't sure we'll use on our pillows? Should we include those things on the list?"

"Ah, good question. Yes, please include everything that you think you may use, and estimate prices like I've explained already. When the project is over, you'll be making a new list and comparing it to the old list—just for fun—to see how closely they match."

The four girls spread their supplies out into piles. Lindsay agreed to act as group secretary and began the list. They spent the rest of the class period getting their supplies figured out and planning ahead for what they wanted to do with their project. They had to be very careful that the other students didn't overhear them talking. Since the girls' pillow project was a secret, the other students were desperately trying to figure it out and went so far as to beg the girls to let them in on the secret. The girls were holding out, though. They vowed not to tell a single person what their pillow was going to be.

Engrossed in their project, the bell rang before any of them realized that class was about to end. They hastily cleaned up their workstation, returned their bin to the appropriate shelf on the wall, and headed off to their respective classes.

"See you at lunch!" they shouted to each other as they raced in separate directions down the hall.

"Mom, I'm leaving for Macy's house," Lindsay called up the stairs when she saw Kelly's mom pull into the driveway to pick her up. She heard some quick rustling, and her mom came bounding down the stairs, making sure she didn't miss Lindsay's exit.

"Now, Linds, let's not have a repeat of last time, okay?"

"Don't worry, Mom. We've agreed that there can be no destruction of private property during our sleepovers." Lindsay laughed.

Mrs. Martin, not finding the comment very funny, became a bit more stern and said, "Lindsay, I am not kidding. You think before you act and be an example to your friends. Okay?"

"Yeah, Mom. I get it. I'll behave," Lindsay promised as Kelly's mom honked her horn. "Gotta go, Mom. Love you." Lindsay gave her a quick kiss and was out the door before Mom could say another word. With a bounce in her step, Lindsay skipped off to the waiting SUV.

When Lindsay and Kelly arrived at Macy's house, they had to wait a moment before pulling into the driveway because Sam's mom was backing out. Kelly's mom rolled into the driveway, and the girls hopped out, grabbing their sleeping bags and pillows as they went.

"Bye, Mom!" Kelly shouted as she closed her door. Her mom nodded and waved as she backed out of the driveway and drove off. The girls rushed up to the door, which was propped open, waiting for them. Slowly, Lindsay pushed it open just a bit more and looked inside. They assumed that Macy and Sam saw them pulling in, so they didn't bother to ring the doorbell. But Lindsay wondered where they had taken off to.

"Hello?" Lindsay tentatively stepped into the house.

"Anyone there?" Kelly stepped in behind her.

"Roar!" Sam and Macy jumped at the other two girls from behind the half wall where they were hiding. Lindsay and Kelly both squealed in shock and then laughed at the silliness. When their heart rates recovered, Lindsay grabbed Macy and Kelly caught Sam, and they tickled the girls until they cried for mercy.

"So what are we going to do first?" Kelly asked when they had all recovered and caught their breath.

"My mom said she'd drop us off at the movie theater if we want to go," Macy replied.

"Hey, that's a great idea," Lindsay responded. "I'm all for that."

"Me, too," Kelly and Sam agreed simultaneously.

The girls opened the newspaper to the movie section and spread it out on the kitchen table so they could select the movie that they wanted to see. It only took a moment to decide because they had already seen two of the options together, so those were naturally out. Several of the other movies had ratings the girls weren't allowed to watch. With two movies left to choose from—a cowboy movie or a romantic comedy—they decided on the comedy.

With only an hour before it was time to leave, all four girls crammed into Macy's tiny but private pink bathroom to get ready. Amid their piles of makeup, hairbrushes, earrings, and perfume, they treated the outing as if they were headed to the prom—"You never know who you might run into," they always said. Sam felt unprepared because she hadn't brought anything special to wear. Undaunted, the girls saw that as an opportunity to plow through Macy's closet in efforts to find something for Sam to wear. They tried several things, but they were all too big for Sam's slight frame. "Okay, okay," Macy gave in. "I have a new shirt that I've been saving for when I lose ten more pounds on my diet. I haven't even taken the tags off it yet. You can wear it if you want to, Sam."

"Really?" Sam squealed. "Are you sure?" Macy assured Sam that she didn't mind and reached far back into her closet to find the shirt. She pulled out a cute little long-sleeved red top with silver buttons down the front and little pockets on the chest. Excitedly, Sam tried it on, and it fit perfectly.

"That movie was funny!" Lindsay said as they laughed and bumped into each other coming out of the theater. They giggled as their eyes adjusted to the light, and they headed toward the food court. The movie ended at eight thirty, but Macy's mom wasn't due to pick them up until nine thirty. Hang out time! With one order of french fries smothered in cheddar cheese and a diet cola to share, they chose their favorite seat on the edge of the food court so they could watch the people go by.

"So, Sam," Macy casually asked, "did you ever ask Tyler's cousin to ask Kenny if he liked me?"

"Oh! I totally forgot to tell you this," Sam leaned forward on her elbows. "I did ask her. She talked to Kenny, and Kenny didn't even have to ask Tyler about you. Kenny told Stephanie that Tyler talks about you all the time and that he has for what seems like years. Kenny also said that he's been trying to get Tyler to make a move forever but that Tyler's just been too shy. What do you think about that?"

Macy tried not to make a big deal out of it, but she couldn't help the grin that quickly spread across her face. "I guess we'll just have to wait and see what happens, then."

"Just see what happens? Are you kidding me?" Kelly was so excited. "You might be the first one of us ever to have a boyfriend. We have to figure out a way to push that boy along a little."

"No, no. I don't want to push him along, because I don't really know what I'm ready for. I mean, what am I going to do? Push him to ask me out only to have to tell him that I can't date? I would be so embarrassed," Macy explained. "I'm just happy to know that he is as interested in me as I am in him. If it took another year to act on it, that would be fine with me."

"I think that's the right way to look at it, Mace," Lindsay said.

"I guess I agree, even though I don't really like it." Sam pouted.

"I totally disagree," Kelly emphatically said. "I think that where there's a will, there's a way. And you'll regret it if you don't pursue this, Macy."

"Well, like I said, it really doesn't matter because he hasn't asked me out, and even if he did, I couldn't go." Macy sighed. "Let's just give it some time and see what happens."

The girls gathered in a circle on the floor for another game of Truth or Dare. This time Lindsay was first. She picked Truth again, and the other three girls groaned.

"Come on, Linds, you have to take a chance in life. What fun is it to do the samething over and over?" Kelly prodded her.

"Yeah," Macy agreed. "You need to walk on the wild side now and then."

"Well, I'll pick Truth this time, but if we play again, I promise I'll pick Dare," Lindsay said, taking the chance and hoping that there might not be a next time.

"Okay." Sam gave in. "As long as you promise. It's no fun for us if you're going to play it safe every time."

"I promise."

"Well then, girls, let's go come up with a good Truth for Lindsay."

The three girls left Lindsay to sit in the circle while they discussed what to ask her for her Truth. While she waited, Lindsay wondered if she was getting herself into a mess. Maybe by giving them a whole week to come up with a good dare, she'd find herself in even more of a predicament than she would have if she had just done it right then. *Oh well,* she decided, *it's too late to worry about that now. It'll be okay.* . . . She hoped.

The girls ran back to the floor and dove into their spots. Since Sam was next in the circle, she got to ask Lindsay her Truth question. "Lindsay, which of the three of us do you like the best?"

"Oh, come on!" Lindsay wailed. "You can't seriously expect me to answer that."

"Oh yes, you have to answer," Kelly replied. "You didn't think we'd make it easy for you, did you?"

Macy just looked on with a nervous expression on her face. "No one will be upset by your answer, Lindsay. But you do need to answer. It's part of the game."

"Fine. You guys asked for it." Lindsay was a little frustrated and figured that they deserved it if they didn't like her answer. "I'll have to say that my answer is Macy. She is the one I've known the longest, and her parents and my parents have been friends for decades. She understands and supports my religion and church commitments, and she deals with the same kind of rules from her parents as I do," Lindsay answered but cut Kelly off before she could interrupt.

"But. . .I'm not finished. Kelly and Sam, you two are my best friends on an equal level with Macy. I could have gone my whole life without answering that question. Since I had to, those were the reasons I chose. I love you all equally, though. *There,* are you happy?"

The three girls collapsed into fits of giggles. They found it amusing that Lindsay was so worried about answering the question. Sam assured her that they knew how she would answer and that it was a logical and fair answer. Kelly wiped pretend tears from her eyes. "It's not like we really care who your favorite is anyway, Lindsay," Kelly said sarcastically and then smiled when she saw the worried expression on Lindsay's face. "Oh, come on now. I'm just kidding."

"Now it's Sam's turn," said Macy, obviously

wanting to change the subject.

"I choose Dare. Judging from Lindsay's question, Truth is no easier than Dare." Sam laughed.

Lindsay, Macy, and Kelly rushed off to come up with a good dare for Sam. They whispered for a few moments, but it didn't take them long. They came back to the circle and told Sam what her dare was.

"Oh, that's no problem at all." Sam jumped up to perform her dare, and the other three looked a little disappointed that she didn't seem to mind it a bit.

Sam went upstairs to Macy's kitchen and, carefully, so that she didn't wake anyone up, took everything out of the kitchen cabinets and put it all neatly back into different cabinets. The glasses that had originally been right next to the sink were moved to the little cabinet over the refrigerator. The plates and bowls that had once been housed over the kitchen counter had switched places with the pots and pans.

Lindsay, Kelly, and Macy watched her in action, giggling. Well, Lindsay and Kelly were giggling, anyway. Macy knew that she'd be the one to have to put it all back the way it had been as soon as her mom tried to find something the next day. But she finally found the humor in the situation when she imagined her mom opening the cabinet to get a coffee cup and finding the blender instead.

"Macy's turn!" Kelly exclaimed as soon as they arrived downstairs after Sam completed the kitchen cabinet dare.

"I pick Dare," Macy said confidently.

"We already know what your dare is, Mace," Lindsay said smugly.

"Oh no. . .what have I gotten myself into?" Macy wailed. "Is it too late to change to Truth?"

"Of course it is." Sam laughed.

Kelly explained Macy's dare to her. "You have to go over to the phone right now and dial Tyler Turner's house. When someone answers or if the answering machine picks up, you have to read what's on this piece of paper. But you can't look at it until it's time to read it."

Macy slumped to the floor in desperation. Having had a crush on Tyler for so long, the thought of embarrassing herself in front of him just made her stomach queasy. "Okay, I'll do it." She crept to the phone and picked up the receiver. As slowly as possible, she dialed the phone and waited for someone to pick up. The answering machine picked up, and Kelly handed her the slip of paper right before the beep.

"Hi, this is Macy calling. I was wondering if Tyler would like to"—Macy gulped and paused before she continued reading—"go on a date with me." She hastily hung up the phone almost in tears from embarrassment. "How am I ever going to face him?" Macy wailed at the girls who couldn't hear her over their own laughter.

When they had finally stopped laughing and Macy had time to think about what she had just done, she complained to the girls. "You guys! I asked you to leave it alone for a while and just wait to see what happens. He's going to think I'm asking him out on a date. And what if he responds that he wants to go out with me? What do I do then?"

"Just take it one thing at a time. It'll be okay, Macy. We just did you a favor. You'll see," Sam promised. After that dare, they admitted that they were tired but had one more Truth or Dare to administer. It was Kelly's turn. "I'm going to pick Truth this time."

Lindsay, Macy, and Sam conferred for a quick minute about what to ask Kelly. Nothing seemed to faze Kelly, so it was tough to come up with a question that would be difficult for her to answer. At Lindsay's prodding, they agreed to go another route on her behalf.

"Kelly," Lindsay began, "you must answer the following question truthfully. Do you already know what dare you will give to me next time, and will it be something horrible?"

Kelly shook her head and laughed. "Okay, you guys took the tired and easy way out, but that's fine. Um. . .yeah. . .I already know what I'll recommend. And, yeah, it will be horrible for you, Linds, but oh so much fun for us." Kelly grinned wickedly at the thought, while Lindsay wondered yet again what she had gotten herself into.

Chapter 7

YOUTH GROUP

Flames were visible through the trees as Lindsay and her dad pulled into the church parking lot just before the start of the first youth group session after the summer break. Knowing that there would be a bonfire that night, Lindsay had planned ahead by bringing a blanket to sit on, a jacket in case it got cool, and some snacks to share with the group. She wore her favorite designer jeans—she only owned one pair of true designer jeans, unlike many of her friends who had several, if not many, pairs—and her best cropped sweater over a white satin cami. Getting out of the car, she felt like a fashionista as she grabbed her things and, as an afterthought, reached into the back to get her

Bible just in case she needed it.

"Bye, Dad! I'll see you at nine."

As her dad backed out of the parking lot, Lindsay took off for the tree line, toward the flames that rose higher and higher as the youth leaders fed more wood into the fire, getting it to roar.

"Hey, guys, need some help?" Lindsay called over to the guys working on the fire as she approached the clearing.

"Whooo-hoooo!" One of them whistled as she approached. "Summer was good to you, Linds."

Lindsay saw that it was Rob calling out to her. He was one of her church buddies whom she'd known since she was four. "Ha, ha, funny, Rob." Lindsay assumed he was teasing her.

"I'm serious, Linds. You look great," Rob continued.

"Well, thanks," Lindsay replied, her cheeks reddening from sudden embarrassment caused by the attention, half wishing she had worn a different outfit but secretly pleased with herself for her choice. She jumped in to help with the setup and got the firewood stacked up and ready to be added to the fire as needed, hoping to avoid any further comments or attention about her appearance.

When it was time to begin, the youth minister, Pastor Steve, took out his guitar to begin the worship time. As the music started, everyone grabbed a seat around the fire. Some sat on the ground; some sat on blankets they had brought from home. Lindsay perched atop a tree stump.

Pastor Steve sat on a log and began to lead the group in some of the fun, rousing choruses that they learned at camp that summer and then some deeper, more soulful choruses to lead them into worship. The music went on for almost an hour but seemed to come to an end fast because of the atmosphere and the feelings of unity and friendship they all felt.

"Let's take this time to share some testimonies of how God blessed us or worked through us this summer," the youth minister suggested after the worship time wound down. "Who would like to go first? How about you, Rob? Would you like to share with us about what you did this summer?"

"Sure," Rob excitedly agreed. "I spent about

six weeks traveling with a medical missions team through Mexico. It was amazing in so many ways. I wouldn't trade the experience for anything, and I can't wait to do it again.

"In specific, I came in contact with hundreds of kids. They were all very sick and needed to be taught better hygiene, better nutrition, and how to use the medications that we provided. There were so many children and adults who needed to be seen that there was no way for the doctors to see them all, so I had to see patients as if I were a doctor. I learned about what to look for and what medication to give, and I would share it with a doctor or nurse and they would approve or change my decision. It was so empowering to be able to have that kind of impact. Life changing, really." Rob finished his testimony, shaking his head at the memories.

"Thanks so much for sharing with us, Rob. Does anyone have questions for him?" Pastor Steve asked the group.

"How did you get involved with this missions team?" Scott asked.

"My parents' friend is a doctor, and he was in charge of putting the teams together. I was there when he was talking to my mom and dad, so I asked if I could do it."

"Will you get to do it again, and how do you think it will affect your future?" Lindsay asked.

"Yes, I will do it every summer that I am able until I am old enough to make a permanent decision about where I feel God is leading me to serve. My future? My future will be in service to God. I can't say for sure that He will have me do this forever, but I would. Whatever He has for me is fine with me."

"You know," the minister interrupted, "this is a good time to share my brief message with you, and then we can go back to testimonies if anyone else has something to share. But Rob's testimony and devotion to serving God is so inspiring to me, and it brings me to a point. What is your life about? What is important to you? Really think about it. Yes, you are all in middle school and high school, and you're young. But who decides what too young is? Does God have age limits?"

He paused between each question to allow the students to consider them. "Rob did very grown-up things this summer in service to God and received untold blessings from the experience.

85

What was your summer about? If you could define it in one word, what would you say the theme of your summer was?" Until that point, the questions hadn't needed an answer, but this time, the minister waited. "Let me rephrase my question. Tell me the one-word theme of your summer."

Lindsay paused for a moment, her heart pounding loudly in her chest, knowing exactly what her answer was. "Me. The one-word theme of my summer was *me*."

"Thank you for your honesty, Lindsay. Such is the truth with most of us. And it's never just our summers. Young people, correct me if I'm wrong." He looked around and made eye contact with the students in order to drive his point home. "The majority of your day, your life is spent focused on your pursuits—education, fun, experiences, material desires. Your basic needs and more are met for you. You don't have to think about where your next meal will come from. You don't have to wonder if you will be able to complete your education. You never wonder if you will receive medical treatment if you need it. With those things out of the way, you are left plenty of time to pursue the things that bring you pleasure. And you do it so well. We all do."

"Well. . . ," Scott interrupted with a perplexed look on his face.

"Yes, Scott, what are you thinking?"

"What are you saying? That we shouldn't be kids, we shouldn't be teenagers, and we shouldn't have the care that our parents give us? Are we wrong for going after an education and saving up for a car and stuff?"

"Well, some questions can only be answered between you and God, because I don't know your heart. But I'm certainly not saying that any of those things are absolutely wrong. But if they are propelled by an entitlement attitude—an attitude that suggests that you *deserve* all of those things—then yes, they become wrong because of that attitude.

The Bible tells us in James, chapter 1, that we should think of it as pure joy when we face hardships and trials because it proves that God is at work in our lives. A few verses later, we're told that it's the people who live humbly who should be proud of their high position and that it's the rich who should be aware of their lowly position.

God doesn't have the same values we do. So if you are seeking His will, you'll be open to whatever He has for you, even if it's not always in line with what you think you want or deserve.

"As Christians, we can't walk through life unaware of the needs around us. We have to realize that, even when we have it so good, many people around us and around the world are suffering. Jesus came to reach those suffering people, and He asks us to partner with Him to do it. We can never be a part of that if our only focus is to drive our own agendas and get what we want all of the time. Our focus has to change from being about us and what we want, to being about Him and where He is working. With that corrected focus, it's a lot easier to live without certain privileges and pleasures, and it's also a lot easier to stay out of trouble. Do you think that if you have the singular focus of serving Jesus and allowing Him to serve others through you that you will make some of the dumb teenage choices you will be faced with? It's impossible."

"So," Steve posed a question, keeping the dialogue flowing, "how do we do it? How do we change our focus and make our lives about everyone but ourselves? And once we know how to do it, we then have to answer the question of whether we want to. What do you think?"

The group remained quiet for a bit as the students considered Steve's words. It was clear that some of them were truly moved by Rob's testimony and Steve's message. Lindsay quietly contemplated her thoughts, and feeling the gentle tug that she had come to recognize as the leading of the Holy Spirit, she opened her mouth to speak but hesitated.

"What is it, Lindsay?" Steve asked. "Go ahead—be honest."

"Well, if I'm to be perfectly honest. . ." She hesitated again.

"It's okay to share openly. Go ahead, Linds," Steve prodded.

"Well, the thing is, I'm in eighth grade. I mean, am I not supposed to think of myself? Isn't that how growing up is supposed to be? But when I hear you talk and I consider Rob's words and what he did with his summer, I know in my heart that you're right, and I realize that Rob found another way. But part of me wishes that I hadn't heard this stuff. To be honest, it's a lot easier to be a kid and to let my parents take care of the details. Expectations from God are the last thing I thought I would have to face right now." Lindsay stopped talking even though she felt like she had more to say. She was conflicted.

"Thank you so much for your honesty," Steve encouraged her. "The reason that you feel so much conflict over this is that your spirit is at war with your flesh. That means that your heart, the part that the Holy Spirit leads, is fighting a battle with the human side of you, the side that Lindsay leads. Believe it or not, it's a good thing. We are told in Galatians, chapter 5, verse 17, 'For the sinful nature desires what is contrary to the Spirit, and the Spirit what is contrary to the sinful nature. They are in conflict with each other, so that you do not do what you want.' Jesus knows that we fight that battle with our humanity, and He encourages us to be victorious through Him. The problem is that it's not just a one-time victory and then it's settled. It's a daily struggle that we must fight. We have to surrender our wills and our desires to Him and choose each day to follow Him."

"Yes," Lindsay jumped in, "that battle you're

talking about, that's exactly how I feel. But I know that I want to serve Jesus and I want to do what He asks me to, but I worry that sometimes I just won't be good enough."

Other students were listening intently, many of them feeling just as Lindsay did.

The youth minister got very quiet as he answered. "Lindsay, the thing is, you won't be good enough."

Everyone looked on in surprise. He had basically told her to give up and forget trying, right? She looked at him for a minute while she considered his words, and he waited before moving on. As soon as he saw the dawn of recognition in her eyes, he began to speak again.

"The beauty of being a Christian is that you will never be good enough. You will fail time and time again. If you could have been good enough, Lindsay, Rob, Sarah, Heather"—Steve looked around the campfire and called off each student's name—"if you had it in you to be good enough for even one day, then you would never have needed a Savior. But thankfully our Father judges us through the blood of His Son, Jesus, if we have accepted Him as our personal Savior.

We aren't judged by what we do; we are judged by what He did. Our actions are always and only a response to the grace we have been shown, never a way to earn that favor. Does that help? Does it maybe take some of the pressure off?"

Lindsay chuckled. "I don't know, maybe it adds pressure in some ways. . .but yes, I see what you're saying. Our acts of service or the choices we make aren't because we're afraid of God and some punishment we might receive; they are because we are in awe of His grace and living for Him in response to it."

"Yes, Lindsay, that's it exactly. I think with that said, we can close in prayer. Is there anyone here. . ."

Lindsay allowed Steve's closing words to trail off as she looked deeply into the fire and considered all that she had heard.

Chapter 8

I DARE YOU

"I don't know if I'm going to Kelly's sleepover tonight, Mom." Lindsay peeked at her mom ro guage her reaction.

"What? Really? Why?" Her mom seemed confused because usually there was nothing more that Lindsay would rather do than hang out with her friends. Noticing Lindsay's discomfort, Mrs. Martin pressed for a bit more information. "Did you girls have a fight or something?"

"No, no, nothing like that," Lindsay assured her. "It's just that. . .well. . .I guess it's nothing." Not wanting to say something she'd regret, Lindsay tried to back out of the conversation. Her mom would have no part of that, though.

"Lindsay, what's going on? You need to be

honest with me so I can help with whatever is troubling you."

"Mom, it's just that sometimes the girls sort of teeter on doing things or saying things that I'm not sure I'm comfortable with. Not bad, really, just enough to make me concerned about where it will all lead. I'm afraid of getting sucked into things that would cause problems." Lindsay squirmed. She felt a lot better after she expressed how she felt, even though it made her nervous. "Mom, I don't want you to think they're bad," she continued, "because they aren't."

"No, Lindsay, I know that they aren't bad. I also know that you are a very good and sensitive girl. It's a wonderful thing that you are concerned about this. Most people don't see trouble coming until it's too late. But recognizing that it's possible isn't enough. You have to decide for yourself what your choices will be when faced with temptation." Mrs. Martin paused to try to read Lindsay's expression.

When Lindsay nodded, her mom continued. "It's not enough to know what right and wrong mean. You have to be strong enough to say no to temptation. Temptations will come throughout all of your life. There is no avoiding them. The problem isn't being tempted; it's what you do when you are. Instead of hiding from it and avoiding your friends, it's better to determine to do what is right and then to be an example of that to the people around you. Does that make sense?"

"Yeah, you're totally right," Lindsay agreed. "It's just hard to be the odd one when your friends are having fun. Especially if it means you get teased."

"Yes, Linds, it is hard. That doesn't change, even as you get older. But just remember a time when Jesus was teased and taunted by the people He thought were His friends. He didn't waver or lose His focus, and He gave His life for those very people who were treating Him badly."

"All right, Mom, I'll go to the sleepover. I wouldn't really want to miss it, anyway. I just wasn't sure what to do."

"You'll be fine, Lindsay. I have faith in you." She reached across the couch and gave her daughter a hug. Lindsay silently hoped that she would be able to live up to her mom's faith in her.

"I'm here!" Lindsay shouted, coming through the gate in the wooden fence and letting it swing shut behind her.

Sam and Kelly were already in Kelly's swimming pool and were having a great time splashing and trying to push each other under the water. Before they even had a chance to respond, Lindsay was already taking off her T-shirt and shorts to uncover the swimsuit she was wearing underneath. She set her bag down, laid her clothes across the back of a chair, and took off for the diving board. She walked out to the end, bounced a few times, and then jumped straight in. After a few seconds, her head popped out of the water, and she sputtered until her face cleared. As soon as she opened her eyes, she was assaulted with waves of water being splashed at her. Kelly and Sam were laughing hard as they attacked Lindsay. She fought back but to no avail. They pushed her under and then let her regain her footing.

Laughing and soaking wet, the three girls got out of the pool and went over to the cooler that Kelly had brought outside for them. Each girl took a soda just as they heard a car door slam in the driveway. Macy had arrived. She came smiling into the backyard, looking fantastic. Her diet had really begun to pay off, and she was picture-perfect in her cute little two-piece swimsuit. "Wow, girl!" Kelly whistled as Macy pushed her sunglasses to the top of her head. "You look great. Who are you trying to impress, though? Him?" Kelly pointed at her ten-year-old brother doing a cannonball off the diving board. They all ducked to avoid the splash and laughed at the suggestion.

"Ha, ha, right!" Macy laughed. "But you never know who you might see."

"I could invite Tyler over for you," Kelly suggested.

"Hey, speaking of him," Sam jumped in, "whatever happened after that phone call you made to his house last weekend?"

"Oh...I don't know...," Macy coyly responded with a twinkle in her eye.

"Come on. What haven't you told us?" Kelly demanded.

"Yeah, you'd better spill it," Lindsay agreed.

"Well, I don't really have anything to report—

unless you'd call the movie we're going to go see Sunday afternoon a piece of information." Macy laughed at their shocked expressions.

"Are you kidding me?" Kelly shrieked.

"You're the first one of us to go on a date," Sam pointed out.

"Wow, I am so impressed," Lindsay and Kelly said at the same time.

"How did you ever get your parents to agree to let you go?" Lindsay wondered.

"It's an afternoon movie, his mom is driving us and picking us up, and it's in a very public place. They really didn't put up too much of a struggle." Macy shrugged. "Believe me, I'm as surprised as you are."

"But the important question is, what are you going to wear?"

"Good question, Kelly. I was going to talk to you about that later. I was hoping you'd let me raid your closet since most of my clothes are too big for me now and they aren't really date-type clothes."

"Oh definitely! We'll figure that out later tonight. For now, let's get to working on that tan of yours." Kelly's brother had gone inside, so the pool was calm and just waiting for them to come back in. They each grabbed a raft and climbed on top to sunbathe.

In Kelly's room, after they had their fill of sun and water, they decided to find an outfit for Macy to wear on her date. "Let's see," Kelly said, digging through her closet, "you have great legs, so let's go for a skirt or shorts."

"I think a skirt will look like I'm trying too hard, so let's try some shorts."

"Oh! What about these?" Kelly held up a pair of very short white denim shorts with a striped belt. "We'll find you a supercute top to go with them."

"There is *no way* those shorts are going to fit me," Macy wailed.

"I'll bet they do fit. You've lost a ton of weight. Try them on," Sam encouraged.

Macy tried on the shorts, and they fit perfectly and showed off her toned and tanned legs beautifully. "Great. Now how about this top?" Kelly held up a hot pink halter top that matched the belt. Macy tried it on and couldn't believe how great she looked. When she came out of the bathroom with the outfit on, the other girls were absolutely speechless. No doubt about it, that was the outfit for her first date with Tyler—her first date ever.

A little while later, after they had eaten, it was time for their game. "Sam, you're first. Truth or Dare?" Macy asked Sam.

"I'll pick Dare," Sam said with a laugh. She was eager to get things going.

The three other girls left Sam on the floor while they conferred over Sam's dare. Scurrying back to the circle, the girls couldn't stop giggling about the dare they'd concocted.

Macy began. "Sam, your dare is to call Pizza Heaven—my brother is working delivery tonight—and order a pizza to be delivered to Stephanie Price's house." The girls giggled because Macy's brother, Zach, had liked Stephanie Price since the third grade. He could barely speak when she was nearby. "Use Stephanie's mom's name so that Zach won't figure out whose order it is until he's on his way to her house."

"Okay, that's easy," Sam replied.

"Wait," Lindsay said with concern. "Who is going to pay for the pizza?"

"That's their problem!" Kelly laughed.

"I don't know. . . ." Lindsay wasn't sure she liked that idea at all.

"Oh, don't be a party pooper." Kelly shrugged. "Besides, your turn is coming soon enough. I'd be more worried about that, if I were you." She finished with a laugh.

Sam had the phone book in her lap, and she'd already dialed the phone, so they all got very quiet and listened. "I'd like to order a pizza for delivery."

"I'd like a large thick-crust pizza, with pepperoni, onions, and anchovies."

At that, the girls found it difficult to control their laughter. Kelly had to leave the room for a second to compose herself while the other girls listened to Sam's end of the conversation.

"Actually, can you make that extra anchovies and extra cheese, too? . . . Please deliver it to 3654 Pennifield Lane. . . . Yes, that's right . . . . Do you take checks? . . . Thank you very much." She hung up the phone and rolled on the floor, trying to stop laughing, so she could tell the girls that the person on the phone had told her it would take just a little bit longer since they only had one delivery person that night. This was great news to the girls since it meant for sure that Zach would deliver the pizza.

Realizing that there was nothing they could do but wait to see if Zach ever tied the prank to them, they moved on with the game.

Macy's turn. "I'll take a Truth."

After a very short conference, the girls knew exactly what they wanted to ask Macy, so they returned to the circle.

"Macy, you must tell the truth. On your date with Tyler this Sunday, exactly what do you hope or imagine could happen? And you must provide *all* of the details that you have thought of, because we know you've imagined what could happen."

"Ugh, I knew it would be about this. Let's see. . . . What do I think will happen?"

"No, not exactly. The question isn't about what you think will happen but what you hope *could* happen," Sam clarified.

"Well, first he'll come to the door and pick me up. My mom and dad will be there, and they'll want to talk to him. I would think his mom would be waiting in the car because she is going to drive us. My dad will probably lecture him on safety and on treating his daughter right, not that there is much that can happen at a movie. From there, we'll leave to head to the mall and his mom will drop us off. We'll go into the movie. I guess that's it."

"Oh no! No way are you getting off that easy. What have you imagined could happen during the movie?" Lindsay asked, getting into the spirit of it.

"Well, I'm sure we'll share a popcorn and maybe even a soda. I guess I hope that we share a soda rather than get our own. It seems more, um, personal that way, if you know what I mean." She paused for a reaction, and the girls nodded, encouraging her to continue. "So then we'll be sitting there, close to each other. Maybe we'll both put our arms up on the armrest at the same time and bump elbows. I'll leave my arm up there and hope he does the same so that our arms are touching."

The girls giggled in nervous embarrassment.

Macy hesitated, not wanting to continue.

"Come on," Kelly encouraged her. "Don't mind us. We're just jealous. Continue."

"The movie will continue for a little while,

and we'll just stay that way, pretending not to notice. Then we'll reach into the popcorn at the same time. I might even wait until he reaches for it and make sure that I do, too. Our fingers will touch."

"Go on," Sam encouraged Macy.

"After that, I really hope he'll hold my hand for most of the rest of the movie. Then—" Macy stopped short, not wanting to finish her sentence, the part they all wanted to hear the most.

"Come on, Macy, you're doing great—don't quit now," Lindsay prodded.

"Yeah, you have to finish your truth," Sam reminded her.

"Well, this next part would probably never happen. This is a first date, and it's in public. But this is about my imagination, so I'll tell you how my daydream ends. We've been holding hands for a long time, and the movie is about to end, which means we'll have to leave the theater and meet up with Tyler's mom. So, he takes a deep breath, leans forward a little bit, and turns toward me. We share a soft, very tender kiss. The lights come on, and it's time to leave." Macy shrugged and pressed her hands to her burning cheeks. "There, that's it. That's the fantasy I have of my first date with Tyler Turner. Now go ahead and laugh."

"No way, we're not going to laugh. I hope it goes just the way you imagined, Macy," Sam said wistfully.

"Are you sure you want to kiss him already?" Lindsay asked, concerned. "Once you have your first kiss, you can't get it back. You want it to be special."

"Oh, it will be," Kelly assured them. "Macy's had a crush on Tyler Turner for so long that he should be her first kiss. No doubt about it."

"I just want her to be sure," Lindsay replied.

"Look at her; she's sure," Sam laughingly replied. Macy was sitting quietly, lost in her daydream, with a soft smile on her face as she imagined what it could be like.

"Kelly, Truth or Dare?" Lindsay asked.

"I'll pick Dare this time," Kelly answered confidently.

The girls conferred about Kelly's dare for quite a while. They were clearly in disagreement over what to choose. Kelly finally spoke up from across the room and said confidently, "Bring me whatever you've got, girls. I can take it." Sam and Macy jumped to their feet, eager to bring their dare to Kelly. Lindsay, with a shrug of her shoulders, reluctantly followed them back to the circle.

"Kelly, you have to drink a can of beer from the refrigerator upstairs—all of it," Sam challenged.

The three girls eyed Kelly expectantly. Surely this would be the dare that would break her and cause the first loss in the game of Truth or Dare.

"No problem!" Kelly jumped up confidently and headed up the stairs to the garage where her dad kept the beer in an old refrigerator. All three girls stared after her with openmouthed expressions. No one could believe that she was willing to do it.

Kelly came back into the kitchen from the garage and headed back downstairs to the basement where she took the can of beer out of the pocket on the front of her hooded sweatshirt. She winked at the girls and popped the can open and began to drink it. Although she tried to chug it down, it was too much for her, and she had to take several breaks. Eventually she was able to empty the can, and just for emphasis, she crushed it in her hand.

"I cannot believe that you just did that, Kelly." Lindsay said incredulously. She shook her head in disbelief.

"How did it taste?" Macy wondered.

"You've never tasted beer?" Kelly asked.

"Nope," Macy replied.

"Me either," both Sam and Lindsay answered. "I tasted a sip of champagne at my cousin's wedding once," Sam added.

"Well, we'll have to change that sometime," Kelly teased, her words slurring a bit from the effects of the alcohol.

"Okay, Lindsay, your turn. And you have to pick Dare, remember?" Macy reminded her.

"Yeah, I know. Just be good to me, guys." Lindsay laughed nervously. She had prepared herself for this, and after seeing what Kelly agreed to do, she figured that her dare couldn't possibly be as difficult. She'd just do whatever it was and get it over with.

The girls huddled for just a moment and then returned to the circle to give Lindsay her dare.

"Lindsay, we dare you to go down to the store on the corner and buy a single can of beer," Kelly looked smug, like she was sure that Lindsay wouldn't do it. "You don't even have to drink it," Kelly added.

"*What?*" Lindsay shouted. "I can't do that! For one thing, we're not allowed to leave the house. For another thing, my parents would have a fit if they knew I went to the store at this hour. And the last straw would be that I bought a can of beer. If I got caught, I would be in so much trouble. That would be the end of our sleepovers, that's for sure."

"Well, let me put it this way," Kelly said, while the other girls sat silently waiting to see what would happen. "If you do it, you will prove that you not only keep your word, based on our deal when this game started, but you will also prove that you really are cool and fun to hang around with. And if you don't do it, you won't be able to be a part of the sleepovers or our group anymore."

Sam and Macy gasped in shock at Kelly's words. "Kelly, that's not what we. . ."

Kelly interrupted her. "Look, we said as a group that we were going to take this game very seriously. Consider it a test of her loyalty."

"But, Kelly, we don't want to put anyone's friendship on the line over a game," Macy pleaded with her.

"It's not just a game. It's a matter of honor. All four of us were there when these rules were decided, and we all agreed to uphold them. If she decides not to, then she has no honor and isn't interested in keeping her word to us."

Sam didn't even try to convince Kelly any longer and turned to Lindsay instead. "Linds, you're not going to get caught. You can just go right out the front door. The store is barely a block away—and if you try to buy the beer and they say no, you still did your part. Right, Kelly?"

"Oh yeah, if she tries but they say no, it's not her fault. We'll even walk with you and watch from outside the window."

Lindsay was about to cry. She didn't want to disappoint her friends, and she wanted to play along and be cool. But this was a big breach of trust, and it was just plain wrong. On the other hand, she would risk losing her best friends if she didn't do it. She didn't think there was anything that she wouldn't do for her friends. She loved her friends and couldn't imagine not having them in her life. But she also couldn't understand how they could sacrifice their friendship over a game. She was so torn over what to do—she felt that she couldn't win either way. But thinking of all their future plans together, she thought that she might lose a whole lot more if she didn't do it. She wished she had more time to decide. They were all staring at her, trying to figure out what she was going to do.

IT'S DECISION TIME

The time has come to make a decision. Think long and hard about what you would really do if you encountered the circumstances Lindsay is facing. It's easy to say that you'd make the right choice. But are you sure that you could stand up to your friends and face their rejection? Once you make your decision, turn to the corresponding page to see how it turns out for Lindsay—and for you.

Turn to page 112 if you think that Lindsay is able to stand up to her friends by refusing to do the dare.

Turn to page 151 if Lindsay is unable to stand up to her friends and chooses to go ahead with the dare.

The next three chapters tell the story of what happened to Lindsay when she decided to do what she knew was right.

Chapter 9

DARING TO BE DIFFERENT

Lindsay's eyes welled up with tears. "I can't do this. I just can't. There's just no way that I would do something this risky that would get me into so much trouble with so many people. Plus, it's not how I operate. I just don't do things like that. I hope you all can just love me for who I am and not for whoever you're trying to make me."

The four girls sat quietly for a few minutes, while Lindsay wiped the tears from her eyes. They were at a sort of crossroads in their relationship. No one was happy that Lindsay decided not to perform the dare, but no one was surprised either. Lindsay picked at the rust-colored fibers of the old couch while she waited for someone to speak. Sam and Macy looked to Kelly and waited for her to take charge, as she usually did at such times.

"Well, first we have to see if someone else is willing to take on the dare. Who is next in the game?"

"It should probably start over with Sam," Macy answered, hoping to avoid the pressure of the dare falling to her.

"Okay, Sam, are you tough enough to take on the challenge of the dare that Lindsay isn't willing to perform?"

"Sure, Kelly, I'll do it for Lindsay," Sam offered, thinking that she was helping.

"Well, you won't actually be doing it *for* Lindsay—you'll be doing it *in place* of Lindsay, who, since she has decided that she is too good for us and our game, has given up her spot." Kelly spoke for the group, making up rules as she went along.

"My spot in the game or my spot in the group?" Lindsay asked hesitantly.

"They are one and the same," Kelly answered coldly, her judgment obviously impaired.

Sam and Macy gasped. This had gotten way too serious. No one wanted to lose Lindsay's friendship, but they *had* made a deal, and Lindsay wasn't playing as an equal.

Lindsay wept openly and tried to make another appeal for herself. "I don't understand why our friendship hinges on me doing something so completely wrong that puts me in danger of getting into lots of trouble. Why don't you all, as my friends, care about what I'm comfortable with and what I'm afraid of? Do I mean so little to you that a stupid challenge is enough to erase all of these years of loyalty and friendship?"

"You're proving your loyalty. Your loyalty is to your stupid rules and your dumb church. I always wondered if they were more important to you than we are, but now I know for sure. "

"No, you're missing the point. I'm not choosing my church and my rules—as you call them, which, by the way, aren't nearly as stupid as the rules you've made up for this game—over you guys. I'm choosing right over wrong, doing the right thing over doing the dare. But if you can't see that, I guess we aren't really the friends I thought we were anyway. How about you, Sam and Macy?" Lindsay asked, wanting to find out exactly where she stood. "Are you in agreement with this?"

At the same moment, both Sam and Macy silently looked away, telling Lindsay just how they felt about it.

"Well, I'm going to call my mom to come and get me, and then you three can continue your fun." Lindsay went to the phone and called home, asking her mom to come and pick her up. She didn't tell her much of the story over the phone, but it was clear from Lindsay's voice that this was very different than a five-year-old calling home because she missed her mommy.

"I'll be right there, Linds."

Lindsay gathered up her belongings: her swimsuit that was still drying over the shower curtain in the basement bathroom, the toothbrush she had left on the vanity, the snacks she had brought to share. . .and she also grabbed a few items that she had left there during past visits. She placed all the items into her backpack and silently walked to the front porch, where she sat on the stoop crying softly while she waited for her mom to arrive.

At just after one in the morning, Mom pulled

into the driveway, and Lindsay rose from the stoop, collected her things, and, with her head down, made the lonely walk to the car. Mercifully her mom didn't say anything on the short drive home because Lindsay was withdrawn, quiet, and not quite ready to talk about what had happened.

When they arrived home, Mom helped Lindsay get her things out of the car and set them on the tile floor in the foyer just inside the front door. Still without saying a word, Mom went into the kitchen and put some water into the teakettle to heat for hot chocolate.

Lindsay washed up in the bathroom and then walked back down the hallway to join her mom. She was hesitant, because she didn't know quite what to say or how much to tell her mom. When she entered the kitchen and Mom looked up at her from the kitchen table, Lindsay started to cry.

"Oh, sweetie." Mom was instantly on her feet and held her daughter as she cried big, sad tears. "Do you want to talk about it?"

"Mom, they—they—they picked a game over me. They didn't have any respect for what I wanted. They don't even know m—m—me, really." Lindsay was crying and not making much sense.

"Slow down, honey. Let's take this one step at a time. Tell me what happened—from the beginning."

"Well, we were playing a game. It started back a few weeks ago when we first started our Friday night sleepovers. The game was a sort of deal that we made. It's called Truth or Dare." Lindsay noticed the look of recognition on her mom's face. "You've heard of it?"

"Linds, everyone has played Truth or Dare. It's not anything new."

"Well, we played seriously. It was a matter of honor to take your turn and either answer the question truthfully or perform your dare with no complaints." Lindsay paused to take a deep breath and blow her nose. "Well, it was my turn, and I picked Dare because they were all mad that I was only choosing Truth." Lindsay started to rush her story, wanting to get it all out as quickly as possible. "My dare was horrible, and I couldn't do it, and they said that if I didn't do it, I was out of the group. But I didn't do it, and so they told me I had to leave, so I called you."

"Okay, slow down. Take a deep breath. What was the dare?"

"I can't tell you yet, Mom."

"Why not? Oh, you mean they still might be doing whatever it is they dared you to do?"

Lindsay nodded, her eyes downcast.

"Lindsay," Mrs. Martin said sternly, "if your friends are in any danger or if they are doing something to endanger someone else, you need to tell me."

"They aren't my friends, and I don't think they're in danger. I'll tell you what they're doing, though," Lindsay pulled a chair out from the table and slumped into it. "I was given a dare, and since I wouldn't do it, they made me leave. But Sam had to take on my dare in my place. She has to leave the house with the other girls following and walk down to the corner store and buy a can of beer. She doesn't have to drink it or anything, just buy it."

Mrs. Martin looked horrified. "Lindsay, first of all, I am very proud of you for having no part in that dare. We'll talk more about that later, though. For now, we have a big problem. Are you aware that not only will they be in trouble with their parents but also with the police? Buying alcohol as a minor is illegal. If they attempt to do it, the shop owner will have to call the police, and they will likely be arrested."

"I thought it was illegal only if we drank it!" Suddenly Lindsay was scared for her friends and worried that something horrible was about to happen.

Lindsay watched her mom pick up the phone. "Mom!"

She held her hand up to Lindsay and began to tell the story to Kelly's mom.

Finishing up her conversation, Mom said, "Well, I just got home. So, since I'm still dressed, I'll head over there right now and see if I can stop this from happening." She hung up the phone and grabbed her purse, cell phone, and keys and headed for the door. As a last thought, she stopped and scribbled a note to Lindsay's dad in case he woke up before they got back. She hurried to the garage, Lindsay scrambling along after her—there was no way she was going to stay home.

They made the short drive back toward Kelly's house and turned the corner to drive to the convenience store. As soon as they made the turn toward the store, they could see the lights. There were two police cars in the parking lot with their lights flashing on top. "Oh no! We're too late!" Lindsay cried.

"Lindsay, it's not your fault that this happened. And maybe getting caught is the best thing that could happen to the girls. They will hopefully learn a lot from this experience. Let's go see what we can do, though." Mrs. Martin parked her car and got out, motioning for Lindsay to stay in her seat. Lindsay didn't argue, because she wasn't in any hurry to see her presumably angry friends, anyway.

From the car, Lindsay could see into the store through the big plate glass front window. She saw her three friends, with their backs against the checkout counter, facing the policeman who stood in front of them, obviously questioning the girls. Lindsay felt so bad for her friends. They didn't know that what they were trying to do was illegal—they did know it was wrong, though.

The three girls turned to face the counters, and the policewoman who had been quiet stepped forward and spoke sternly to the crying girls. Mom approached them and tried to reason with the police but was motioned to step back and stay out of the situation. Because she wasn't one of the girls' mothers and she didn't have a child involved in the prank, there was nothing she could do but use her cell phone to call their parents.

Since Kelly's mom was already on her way, Mom dialed Sam's home first. Sam was in the most trouble because she was the one who had actually asked for the beer. Lindsay watched her mom cry as she told Mrs. Lowell the story. There was nothing left to say, so she hung up the phone and called Macy's house.

Lindsay sat in the car, quietly praying for her ex-friends, worried about the trouble that they had gotten into and what would happen to them—and to their friendship.

Back in the Martins' cheery kitchen, Lindsay felt anything but cheerful as she sipped her reheated hot chocolate. She impatiently waited for her mom to finish her phone conversation so she could find out what had happened to her friends.

"Lindsay," her mom started hesitantly after she hung up the phone, "that was Kelly's dad. Her mom was too upset to answer her cell phone.

It seems that they are going to make examples of the girls. Sam is in trouble for attempting to purchase alcohol, and Kelly is in even bigger trouble for consuming alcohol. They discovered that she drank an entire can of beer. I thought you said that there was no drinking involved?"

Lindsay buried her head in her hands and sobbed. She was so sad and scared for her friends but also relieved that she had avoided, though narrowly, this trouble for herself. Between her tears, she attempted to answer her mom. "There was no drinking involved in my dare, but Kelly's dare was to drink an entire can of beer from her parents' refrigerator. I should have stood up to them then. Maybe this whole thing could have been avoided." She continued to cry, shaking her head.

"Sweetie, there are a lot of things about tonight that I wish had gone differently. But one thing I am confident of is that I am so proud of you for taking the stand you did. Whether it should have been sooner or could have been done differently isn't the question. Each one of you girls is responsible for—and will have to pay for—your own actions. In your case, you've only made me more proud of you and more confident in your trustworthiness. You faced some very difficult and very adult decisions tonight, Lindsay, and you did the right things even though they were very hard. In fact, it's because your choices were so hard that they are so honorable.

"I know it seems pretty bleak right now. Not only do you feel like you lost your best friends, but you still love them and know that they are suffering right now." Lindsay was crying so hard that her shoulders were shaking. "Lindsay, honey, it's going to be okay."

"I know, Mom, I'm just so. . .relieved. And I feel guilty about that. But I am so glad that I did what I did."

"I have an idea. Let's pray for the girls right now."

"Okay, Mom."

"Father in heaven, thank You for keeping all four of these girls safe tonight. Thank You for giving Lindsay the strength and confidence she needed to withstand the pressures that she endured from the other girls. Please protect those three girls and help them to learn a valuable lesson from all of this, and please help Lindsay to continue to be used as a witness for You in the midst of this tragedy. Amen."

"Amen."

Chapter 10

OUT OF THE CLUB

The walk into the school was a very lonely one for Lindsay. She kept her head down and put one foot in front of the other until she found herself at her locker. She didn't want to see if her friends were talking near their favorite tree—and she especially didn't want to see if they weren't. Kelly and Sam weren't taking calls from Lindsay, and Macy wasn't allowed to come to the phone, so Lindsay didn't have any new word on what had happened on Friday night.

Without looking around at the students milling in the halls, she slowly gathered the things she would need from her locker for her first class. She wasn't in any hurry to get to class, so she stood there for much longer than she actually needed to.

"Hey, can I talk to you for a minute?" a male voice said from right behind her left ear.

Lindsay jumped with a startled squeal and turned to face Tyler Turner, who stood at her locker with a sad look on his face. He wore his typical outfit: baggy jeans and a baseball T-shirt with a ball cap on his head. But today, somehow he just looked dark. His black jeans and dark gray T-shirt along with the black baseball cap seemed to match the expression on his face: dark and sad.

"Yeah, sure, what's up?" Lindsay was pretty sure she already knew what he wanted to talk to her about.

"Um, well, Macy and I were supposed to have a movie date yesterday, but she didn't answer her phone, didn't answer her doorbell, and never called to tell me what happened. It's almost as if she just completely blew me off. Did I do something to upset her?" Tyler looked perplexed and genuinely concerned.

"You mean you haven't heard what happened?" Lindsay asked with disbelief.

"No, I haven't heard anything." Tyler seemed to realize all of a sudden that something could actually have gone wrong. "Is Macy hurt? Is she okay?" he asked frantically.

"Yes, Macy is fine. She's in quite a bit of trouble and was probably not allowed to use the phone. I'm going to be late to class, and I don't really want to talk about it. Just know that she'll be okay, and she'll fill you in on the details when she's ready. And, um, her part in the trouble isn't as bad as it could have been, if that helps at all." She turned immediately to leave, hoping to escape without any more questions.

"Wait, I just need to know one more thing," Tyler begged, needing reassurance. "Before this thing happened, was she excited about our date?"

"Yes, Tyler, she was very excited. I promise you that." At that moment, the bell rang and the two parted ways without saying another word.

The first class of the day wasn't too bad, but by second period, word had started to get around and kids were looking at Lindsay with funny expressions. She could feel their stares as she walked down the hall. She was sure that some of them would make fun of her for leaving the girls' party. But at that point, she didn't care.

The worst moment came when she had to

enter home ec. Knowing that it was the final week to work on their project in class, Lindsay was dreading what was sure to be a very awkward and uncomfortable hour. But they had to complete their project so it could be presented to the class the next week.

Standing outside the classroom, waiting until the last second before the bell rang to slip in, hoping to avoid the awkward silence before class started, Lindsay said a quick prayer. Just as the bell was about to ring, she walked in with her head held high. She noticed that none of her friends were in their seats. She hadn't seen them all day, but she had thought that they must be avoiding her, not that they were absent. She became very worried and approached her teacher. "Mrs. Portney, I don't think any of my group members are here. Are they sick or something?"

"Well, Lindsay, I don't think it's that they're sick. I am sure you're aware of some of the circumstances from the weekend." When Lindsay nodded silently, Mrs. Portney continued. "They are on a school suspension for a short time until the administration decides what needs to be done."

"Oh, I see." Lindsay slumped back to her seat and sat at their big table all by herself. She quietly spread the craft items in front of her after deciding to go ahead and finish the project on her own. She got lost in her work until the bell rang, and without a word to anyone else, she packed up and left for lunch, where she also sat alone. It was becoming too much to bear. The loneliness. The worry. The fear. The embarrassment. She felt her eyes welling up with tears, so she escaped to the hallway where she could use the phone to call her mom.

"Mom, it's horrible!" Lindsay cried into the phone. "The kids are all staring at me, and Sam, Macy, and Kelly aren't even in school today. They're suspended. What's happening to them?"

"Slow down, sweetie. I know you only have a few minutes, so just listen to me. The girls are fine. I've spoken to Mrs. Lowell and Mrs. Monroe. Yes, they are suspended for three days, but they'll be back in school on Thursday. And yes, they are in trouble at home, of course, and will have a punishment to deal with for quite a while, I would imagine. We aren't sure yet what the legal situation will be, but these are young girls who have never been in trouble before. Whatever happens, they can and will get through it. The important thing for you to remember, Linds," Mom stressed, "is that you did the right thing. Let things play out now, and they will work out. Everything has a way of working out. Use this to build your reputation. Don't slink away because of it. Use it as part of your witness for Jesus, or it will be all for nothing. Just hold your head up high, and show your confidence."

"Okay, Mom. That really helps. I'm going to do it. At least now I don't have to worry so much about what's happening to the girls. I have to go now—the bell's about to ring."

"Bye, Lindsay. I love you."

"I love you, too, Mom."

The week crept by while Lindsay waited for her friends to come back to school. On one hand, she couldn't wait to see them, to see if they were really okay; but on the other hand, she dreaded facing the fact that they really wanted nothing to do with her. One thing she knew for sure: She was really looking forward to being out of the limelight and past the whispering stage. The other kids were so curious about what had happened that they either came right out and asked Lindsay every chance they got, or worse, they whispered behind her back and speculated about what might have happened.

The most difficult part of the week was continuing with the pillow the group had been making for home ec class. It was supposed to be a group project, but Lindsay had to finish it by herself. She asked Mrs. Portney if there was anything else she could do, but her teacher urged her to continue and use the class time wisely. So the pillow was almost complete. Lindsay was hoping that on Thursday the other girls would be able to put some personal finishing touches on it—if they would even speak to her.

On Wednesday afternoon, Lindsay went home right after school, as had been the pattern all week long. She sat in the family's formal dining room to complete her homework. Distracted by the birds being chased by a squirrel in the backyard, Lindsay stared out the large, plate-glass bay window.

As her thoughts wandered, she didn't hear the

sound of a car pulling into their long driveway, nor did she hear the doorbell ring. Moments later, Mrs. Martin escorted a very timid Macy into the dining room. "Sweetie, someone is here to see you. I'll leave you two to talk, and Mrs. Monroe and I will be in the kitchen having a cup of coffee."

Lindsay was silent as she looked at her friend. She willed herself not to cry but was quickly losing the battle. The tears started to form, and knowing there was nothing she could do about it, she let them fall.

Macy ran to her side and hugged her. "Lindsay, I am so sorry. Can you ever forgive me?" Macy begged.

"Of course I can, and I do. I missed you. I miss all of you."

"I know, Linds. I just can't believe that things turned out like they did. Kelly and Sam got into so much trouble. I am just in trouble at home, not with the police—but it's bad enough. My mom is here because she knew I needed to talk to you, but she's only giving me a few minutes. She is disappointed in me for the way I treated you. I'm just so sorry, Lindsay."

"Look, Mace, remember that talk the school counselor gave last year about peer pressure and how it's easy to get caught in the moment? It's that way with Sam and Kelly. They have a way of persuading us to do stuff, knowing we'll go along with them just because we want to make everyone happy. I'm not saying that makes it okay, just that's the way it is. Since this happened, my mom and I have talked a lot about how the decisions we make now—and how we learn from them—will help shape who we will become as we grow up. Give yourself a break. We all make mistakes, but we need to learn something and try not to make them again. It doesn't mean the world is coming to an end. It also doesn't mean I don't want to be your friend."

"But—but," Macy stuttered as she fought through her own tears, "I let them make fun of you—I let them kick you out of the group. How can you forgive me so easily?"

"Oh, Macy, no one's perfect. It's like my youth pastor is always saying: We're all imperfect, all sinners, but God freely offers forgiveness to us through the sacrifice of His own Son. If Jesus gave Himself to die so I could be forgiven for my sins, how can I not forgive you? The Bible says that once God forgives us, He forgets about our sins. So what do you say we just forget about this?"

"Oh, Lindsay, I'm so glad to hear you say that, and you're so right. But I can't forget about this. It's going to be going on for a long time, just eating at me."

"Well, I wasn't meaning that we should forget about the consequences," Lindsay explained. "They have to be faced. But our friendship can be healed. We can put that part of it behind us right now."

"I'd really love that, Lindsay."

"Done." The girls laughed together and both breathed a deep sigh of relief.

"Just remember what I told you about God's forgiveness. It's a free offer. You know that."

"I know, and I think I'm starting to understand how that works."

Macy's mom came into the room and told her that it was time to go. Macy and Lindsay would see each other at school the next morning. Macy asked Lindsay if she would be waiting by the tree.

"Um, no," Lindsay answered. "There are other things that have to be taken care of before that can happen. I'll just be in the school getting ready for class. I'll see you in home ec, though."

As Macy and her mom were getting ready to leave, Mrs. Monroe paused with her hand on the brass doorknob. "Lindsay, I just wanted to tell you that I am very proud of you, and I am grateful for your influence in Macy's life. I heard a lot of what you said in the dining room, and, well, I'm just very proud of you."

They left without waiting for a reply, and Lindsay quietly shut the door behind them. She turned to find her mom standing there, watching her, softly smiling. Lindsay took a step toward her and was immediately engulfed in motherly, comforting arms. Healing had begun.

Thursday morning came too quickly for Lindsay. She dreaded the walk into the school and the effort it would take to avoid Kelly and Sam. It would also be difficult to see Macy with Sam and Kelly, but she had to let Macy find her own way through the confusion.

She dressed carefully—not wanting to appear

too eager but also not wanting to look like she didn't care. She chose to wear the same outfit that she wore to school on the first day, hoping that since they helped her pick it out, it might make the other girls feel nostalgic for a time when things were much less complicated.

With her backpack slung casually over one shoulder and her head held high, Lindsay walked into the school a full ten minutes before the time that she usually met the girls under the tree in the school yard. She got what she needed from her locker and then slipped into her first-period classroom, choosing a desk near the window where she could look out onto the yard unnoticed.

The school bus pulled up to the curb, and students began to file off with their piles of books and backpacks. The last three to exit the bus were Macy, Sam, and Kelly who, for some reason, all rode the bus that day. They were laughing and looking as though they hadn't a care in the world. They sauntered over to their tree and casually leaned against it while they talked and laughed. Lindsay looked on from her desk at the window, amazed that they seemed so carefree. Then she noticed that Sam and Kelly were both wearing dark sunglasses and Kelly had a hat on her head. They were hiding in their own way, while trying to look at ease.

At that moment, Kelly turned and noticed Lindsay watching from the window. She nudged Sam and pointed at the school, whispering something to her. They both stared at Lindsay for a moment and held her gaze before they looked away in disgust. Lindsay was heartbroken but could not tear her eyes away from the scene. The three girls started to walk into the school, Macy last. She looked at Lindsay with pity and longing, wishing that things could be very different—but they weren't. They had created this situation; now they had to face it.

Chapter 11

MAKING AMENDS

Well before class was to start, Lindsay walked into the home economics room and asked Mrs. Portney if there was something else she could do during the class period to give Macy, Sam, and Kelly a chance to work on their project alone since they had missed so many days. In truth, Lindsay wanted to avoid having to work with them and thought that just missing the class entirely was a good option. Mrs. Portney understood that there was a problem going on, so she wisely said that it just wasn't an option. She asked Lindsay to stay in class and face up to her challenges. She recommended that Lindsay just be bigger than the problem, act maturely and confidently, and show that she was not bothered by any of it.

As Lindsay was leaving the room to visit her locker before the bell rang, resigned to do as her teacher asked, Mrs. Portney stopped her so that she could make one last comment. "Lindsay, I just wanted to tell you that I think I've heard enough of the story of what went on last weekend to confidently say that I'm very proud of you for your strength of character and your willingness to defend your principles. You did the right thing, and everything will work out better than you could even imagine. Now go ahead, and get your things."

Lindsay nodded and ducked out of the classroom. She gathered the few books she needed for her afternoon classes and headed back to the home ec room. As she arrived, she saw that Kelly, Sam, and Macy were entering the classroom just ahead of her. She took a deep breath, straightened her shoulders, held her head up high, and confidently walked into the classroom. She walked to her seat and calmly sat next to her friends. Macy quietly caught her gaze from across the table and gave her a slight wink, just enough to boost Lindsay's confidence and convince her that she was doing well.

"Settle down, class. Let's quiet down and pay

attention." Mrs. Portney waited until the class had stopped talking before continuing. "This is the very last class period that you have to work on your projects, so please use the time wisely. Tomorrow will be the day for you to present your projects to the class and share your findings and cost comparisons. Now, get to work."

"I set it up with Mrs. Portney just before class," Kelly immediately jumped in, avoiding all small talk. "We can take our things to the library and work on our pillow there so that we can keep it a surprise from the class." The four of them gathered their things and quietly left the classroom. No one knew quite what to say. Lindsay broke the ice.

"I don't want this to be uncomfortable. If you guys want, since I did a lot of work on the pillow while you were out of school, I can just read or something while you three finish up the pillow."

"No way!" Macy would have none of that. "We started this together—we'll finish it together."

Sam and Kelly had looked like they had been about to go along with Lindsay's plan, but when Macy made her statement, they reluctantly agreed. "Besides, it could affect your grade if you don't participate, Lindsay," Macy continued.

To that, Kelly rolled her eyes. "Not like she'd risk getting into trouble."

Lindsay took a deep breath. Enough was enough. "I just have to say this, and then we can do our work. Kelly, you're selfish. You want things just how you want them, and if anyone goes against you, you have no use for her. I am a person, too. I have plans, feelings, emotions, limits, likes, and dislikes, just like you do. I also have the capability to make a decision about what I want for myself. If you ever hope to have a real friend and not just a follower, then you'll have to learn to appreciate the differences in people and give others room to be themselves. Otherwise, rather than real friends, you'll always only have people around you until they are tired of just following your orders and taking your bullying."

Kelly stared at her with her mouth open. No one had ever spoken up to her that way. Sam spoke up. "Hold on, Lindsay, I take offense to that. Are you saying that I am just a follower and can't make up my own mind?"

"Well, think about it, Sam. That whole night,

all of the dares—they were Kelly's idea. When I refused, it was Kelly who demanded that I be cut out. You and Macy didn't want to, but you went right along with Kelly. Macy at least had the guts to come to me and apologize."

Kelly glared at Macy when she heard that.

"See?" Lindsay whispered emphatically. "It makes you crazy mad, Kelly, to think that Macy came and apologized to me, that she would want to be my friend even though you said she couldn't."

Macy tentatively opened her mouth. "You know what? I agree with Lindsay completely. I don't want to be a follower. I want to be my own person. My heart tells me that Lindsay is one of my best friends, and I'm not willing to turn my back on her just to follow the orders of another one of my best friends. I think that you need to do some soul-searching, Kelly, and decide what you want out of your friendships and if you're willing and able to respect us as people and appreciate our differences rather than try to erase them."

Sam had been quiet for a while, but it seemed like some of the things she was hearing had gotten to her. She quietly said, "I'm sorry,

Lindsay; you're totally right. I'm sorry for how I've been acting. Can you forgive me?"

"Of course I can, and I do. It's over and done."

"Well, if you three are finished, we have some work to do." Kelly was having no part of the apologies and wanted to change the subject.

Lindsay showed them what she had done to their pillow while they were out of school. There wasn't a whole lot of work that remained, so Kelly, Sam, and Macy set about to complete the pillow while Lindsay worked on finalizing the cost and material comparison report. The four girls finished their work at about the same time, and they sat back to survey the results.

All four of them laughed when they stepped back to really look at their finished pillow. It looked just like Mrs. Portney. To prove it, Sam took the pillow up to the circulation desk and asked the librarian, Mrs. Woods, to look at the pillow and see if it reminded her of anyone.

Mrs. Woods looked up from the book she was reading and lowered her glasses so she could peer over the top of them at the pillow in Sam's hands. Immediately she started to laugh. "Well,

I'll be. It's a Portney Pillow." She laughed until she had to wipe the tears from her eyes. After she composed herself, she said, "You girls have done a great job on that pillow. It looks just like her down to the littlest details. Great job."

Confidently the four girls headed back to class to get everything put away before the bell rang. Their Portney Pillow was carefully wrapped in plastic and stowed in their bin, awaiting the day they could reveal it. They gathered their things and readied themselves to head off to their next class. Lindsay, trying not to be too intrusive, moved to leave immediately so that the others could walk together.

Kelly reached out and grabbed her backpack and softly tugged her back. "Linds, just give me some time to figure things out. I heard everything that you said, and I'm not a completely coldhearted person. I just need some time. But you don't need to leave. You didn't do anything wrong. I just have to figure out what I did wrong." With that, Kelly left alone, leaving Sam, Macy, and Lindsay to stare after her, dumbfounded.

"Wow, I guess miracles can happen," Macy said.

"Pray, girls. Just pray," Lindsay encouraged them.

❋

As Lindsay woke up Friday morning, she thought she heard the phone ringing, but it was hazy. A few moments later, there was a knock at her door and her mom was standing there holding the cordless phone. "Lindsay, it's Macy on the phone for you."

Lindsay groggily sat up in her bed and reached for the phone while rubbing her eyes as they adjusted to the bright sunshine streaming through the windows. "Hello? Macy?"

"Hey, Linds, I just wanted to catch you before you left for school. I know that you've been trying to get there early so you can go hide out in your classroom." She hesitated as she chose her next words carefully. "I just. . . I guess I just don't think that's fair. Sam and I want you to come to our tree. There's nothing that you should be hiding from. You didn't do anything wrong."

"Macy, I really appreciate that you're concerned about this, but I really don't want to cause any more problems. I really want to give Kelly the time that she asked for and see what happens without pushing it."

"I know, Lindsay, and I can respect that, but I

also think that if we don't all show Kelly that we aren't going to accept things as they are, it won't make her sit up and take notice. She needs to realize that it's not her call. She can take the time she needs, and we're all there for her, but she can't control us in the process."

"Okay, here's what I'm going to do, Mace," Lindsay explained. "Since I'm up so early and now have plenty of time before school"—both girls laughed—"I'm going to talk about it with my mom and pray about it. I just want to do the right thing and not mess up any progress that we've already made."

"Lindsay, I think that's a great idea," Macy agreed. "You know, I think you're the wisest person I know."

"Thanks, Mace. I'll see you at school one way or another."

Lindsay decided that she needed to approach Kelly alone so she didn't feel bombarded by all of them at once. So she went to another tree and waited there. The tree in Kelly's front yard seemed to be the perfect place. Kelly would see her standing there when she came out to walk the dog before she and her mom left for school. So Lindsay waited.

After about five minutes, the front door opened and Kelly appeared in the entrance, struggling with their golden retriever, Abby. She started to walk out to the front yard but stopped short when she saw Lindsay waiting there. "Hey," Kelly said without emotion. She tried to pretend she wasn't interested in talking to Lindsay.

"Hey, Kell. I thought it was time that we talked. Don't you think this has gone on long enough?"

"Yeah, I guess so. Where do we go from here, though? I mean, how can we possibly fix this?"

"Well, the way I see it, I've already told you the ways I feel I've been hurt. Now you can respond to that if you want to. And if I have done anything to hurt you, this would be the time for you to tell me."

"See, that's the thing, Lindsay. You're perfect. You haven't done anything wrong, and you never will. I can never measure up to you. You'll always be strong enough to be your own person."

"What is it about that that scares you? Is it because you can't control me? So what? It's not a competition. I love you for who you are, and I don't want to change you. Why do you want to change me?"

Kelly began to cry. "I know that's how you feel, but it's easy for you. You have nothing to worry about. You don't care if people like you or not—but they always do, because you're perfect. It's different for me. Before you girls, I didn't really have best friends. I guess I was afraid— afraid that when you said you liked Macy best of all of us, it meant the two of you might go off and just be friends without me and that Sam would go with you because she likes you better. I thought if I kicked you out, they'd stop liking you."

"But, Kelly, don't you see, maybe that's the reason you feel like you never had friends before us. I love you for who you are, and yet you still pushed me away instead of just letting us love you and trusting that we can each do our own thing and still stay friends."

"You're right, Lindsay. . .you're totally right. I'm so sorry. Can you ever forgive me?"

"It's already done, Kelly. And someday, maybe I'll be able to tell you about real forgiveness. For now, we need to get to school and put this behind us. Deal?"

They hugged in Kelly's front yard, and Lindsay just held Kelly while she sobbed some cleansing tears that celebrated the freedom in forgiveness.

The next three chapters tell the story of what happened to Lindsay when she decided to give in to peer pressure by going through with the dare.

Chapter 9

I'LL DO IT

The minutes seemed like a lifetime as Macy and Sam waited for Lindsay to decide. Kelly, feigning disinterest, picked at her fingernails while she waited. She looked up after a minute or two and said, "Well, this isn't that difficult of a decision. You're either in, or you're out. What's it going to be?"

"I can't believe I'm saying this, but I'll do it. Let's just go and get it over with—fast!" Lindsay got up immediately, and her surprised friends followed her up the stairs. She hurriedly slipped on her sandals and quietly opened the front door, hoping it wouldn't squeak. One by one, each girl slipped through the open door, and then, making sure it wasn't locked, Lindsay carefully and silently closed it.

They giggled as they walked down the sidewalk toward the convenience store—everyone but Lindsay. She was so nervous that she spent the entire walk fighting off tears.

"Hey, Lindsay," Kelly said, "you've got to pull it together. If you go in there looking like that, you'll never be allowed to buy the beer. You need to look confident and carefree—not like you're facing a firing squad."

"You're right," Lindsay said, laughing. "I can do this. It'll be fine. I won't get caught. It's almost over. . . ." She recited encouragement to herself, hoping it would boost her confidence.

They arrived at the store much too soon for Lindsay's comfort, but she did just want to get her task over with and then get back safely to the comfort of Kelly's house as fast as possible.

The three girls walked over to the large windows where they could peer between the advertisements and signs to watch Lindsay as she carried out her dare. Lindsay walked up to the door, took a deep breath, squared her shoulders, and opened it. The door swung toward her with the jingling of bells that hung from the top of the door to alert the shopkeeper that a customer was entering the store. He was behind the counter reading a newspaper and looked up for only a second to notice Lindsay. Apparently she didn't look like much of a threat because he went back to reading his paper.

Lindsay considered heading straight for the refrigerator cases at the back and getting it over with but decided that she would be more believable if she shopped for a few other items first. So she wandered down the aisles and selected a loaf of bread, a pack of gum, a bottle of water, and then went to get her can of beer. She opened the door to the cooler where the single cans were stored, and without checking the price or brand, she just grabbed the closest one to her and let the door swing shut. It bounced off the frame with a bang that startled both Lindsay and the shopkeeper, who put his newspaper down to keep an eye on her.

Remembering that it didn't matter if the clerk allowed her to buy it or not, Lindsay figured that it was safe to make her purchases. She stood up very straight as she walked to the cash register, hoping that she looked much older than her age. As she approached the clerk, she had a great idea—so she thought. She would tell the cashier that the beer was for her dad. That way he wouldn't be so hesitant to sell it to her. After she placed her items on the counter, she took out her wallet.

Without even looking at the items he was scanning, the clerk put them into the bag one at a time. Lindsay hoped that he wouldn't even notice the beer. He picked up the cold can to scan it but looked down first. With a small gasp, he looked from the can of beer to Lindsay and then back to the beer. He opened his mouth to speak, but Lindsay interrupted, "Oh, don't worry, it's for my dad. He sent me down here to pick that up for him." The clerk looked at her for a moment, clearly not sure what he should do.

"Okay, give me just one second. I'm out of the right kind of bags up here. A paper bag won't work for a cold can. It will just break right through." He hustled toward the back room.

Lindsay was so relieved. It looked like everything was going smoothly, so she turned to give the girls a thumbs-up. They were still staring through the window, and Kelly was smiling smugly. She was clearly surprised and pleased that Lindsay had carried out her dare.

The shopkeeper slowly walked from the back room with his arms full of bags. Once back at the cash register, he began to stock the bags of all sizes into their respective bins. "Sorry, I just figured that since I was back there, I'd grab some of each size."

"Oh, it's all right," Lindsay said, clearly relaxing. "I'm not in any hurry."

At that very moment, Lindsay noticed a lot of activity at the front window and turned to see what was happening. A police car pulled into the parking lot with its lights flashing and the siren off. Two policemen exited the car; one went over to where Sam, Kelly, and Macy were standing, and the other one headed for the front door of the store.

"What's going on?" Lindsay asked the shopkeeper in a panic. Were the police there for her?

"You kids need to be taught a lesson," he sputtered back at her.

Both policemen had entered the store and were eyeing Lindsay as they asked the clerk what the trouble was. He told them that she had been attempting to purchase alcohol. He had called because he was tired of kids trying to get away with this and knew that he could get into a lot of trouble if he sold it to her.

"You did the absolute right thing by calling us," one of the policemen assured him. "So, miss, what is your name, and how old are you?"

"M–m–my name is Lindsay," she stammered. "I'm thirteen."

"Wow, they just get younger and younger, don't they?" The policeman asked his partner, who agreed emphatically.

"But, officer," Lindsay shakily tried to explain, "I didn't do anything wrong. I wasn't going to drink the beer. I just had to buy it for a dare. I would never have actually drunk it."

"It doesn't matter. You are a minor, and even attempting to purchase alcohol has a penalty of a huge fine and all kinds of other legal problems," the officer said. If he were trying to scare her, it worked. "This is very serious. I'm going to need to get some information from you."

The policeman asked some questions that Lindsay answered, but she was having a difficult time focusing on his words. Her thoughts were swimming, and she began to panic. Then she noticed that her friends were being loaded into the back of a squad car by the other policeman.

"Where are you taking my friends?" Lindsay wiped at the streaming tears on her cheeks. She was alone in her trouble. Even Kelly, who had drunk a whole can of beer, had waited outside with the others while Lindsay carried out her dare alone, so she had escaped close scrutiny from the police.

"They are being taken home. The officer will speak to their parents, but they aren't in any trouble—other than whatever their parents deem appropriate for them being out so late, of course. You, on the other hand, will be accompanying me to the station."

Lindsay began to weep, her shoulders shaking under the enormity of the situation. How could she have gotten herself into this mess? What was she thinking? Suddenly the words hit her: "Sin creeps in silently, slowly. . . ."

The officer led her to the black-and-white squad car and helped her into the backseat. Mercifully he chose not to use handcuffs, although he could have, he told her. She endured the short ride to the police station in silence, sure that her parents would be there waiting for her when she arrived. Pulling into the parking lot, however, Lindsay didn't see their car. On one hand, she was relieved because the thought of facing them was just too much for her to bear. But on the other hand, she felt so alone and vulnerable walking into the police station led by one policeman and followed by another. She was under arrest, and no amount of wishing or begging was going to make this go away.

Lindsay was led to a seat in a small room where a policewoman was sitting at a desk, ready to take down her information. "Lindsay, I'm not going to question you about the crime until your parents are here, but I do need to get some information from you and process you before they will be allowed in."

She began to ask Lindsay questions like her name, her parents' names, her address, where she went to school, how old she was, and how many siblings she had.

The questions continued for a long time with no thought or concern for the tears falling down her face. It wouldn't have mattered, anyway; there was no way she could have controlled her tears. She answered the questions as best she could, but mostly her thoughts were consumed with dread over the moment when her parents would arrive. She wanted them to be there to comfort her, but she couldn't stand the thought of seeing their disappointment and anger.

She was taken back to her seat and told that Officer Marshall was talking with her parents and would bring them in to see her in a moment. Lindsay's heart sank at the very thought of facing them. She could never have imagined how painful regret would be. It was like a knife driving through her heart. What she wouldn't give to go back and do the whole thing all over again. She would have made a far different choice. But it was too late.

She heard a door open and then slam shut, the lock sliding into place. Lindsay listened with dread to the sound of hollow footsteps on the tile floor until they stopped at the doorway to her holding room. She looked up and, at that moment, felt the agony that was visible on her mother's swollen, tear-streaked face. She looked as though a loved one had died—in some ways, one had. Her dad was stone-faced, emotionless, in shock. He clearly didn't know how to react or what to do.

"Should we have a lawyer here?" he asked Officer Marshall.

The officer informed her parents that no questioning had taken place yet, so they were free to call an attorney if they wished. But, the officer also promised, if they began the questioning process without the attorney, they could stop at any time should they decide to call one. He assured them that he just wanted to sort out the details and then they could be on their way.

"Well, let's just get to the bottom of this thing, then," Lindsay's dad said quietly, resigned to the fact that this was not going to be enjoyable for any of them.

"Lindsay, I'm going to turn on this tape recorder now. It just saves me from having to write a lot of notes." When Lindsay nodded, the officer continued. "Let's just make this a bit easier on all of us. Rather than me peppering you with all sorts of questions, why don't you just tell us what happened?"

Lindsay, grateful to be able to tell her side of the story, started at the very beginning, with the first sleepover and the first time they played Truth or Dare. When she finished her story, her mom had finally stopped crying and was able to speak. "Lindsay, what you've done is very wrong. Aside from the many, many ways that you broke our rules and the rules at the Garretts' home, didn't you realize that attempting to buy alcohol was illegal?"

"No, Mom, I had no idea. I knew it was illegal to drink it. But I never knew it was illegal to even buy it. I told the shopkeeper that my dad had sent me to the store for it, so I thought he would sell it to me since it wasn't for me."

"So on top of all of the rules *and* laws you broke, you lied and risked your father's reputation. You know how we feel about alcohol. To think that your dad would drink that beer, let alone send *you* to the store to buy it—it's awful." Her head in her hands, she continued. "Oh, Lindsay, what I wouldn't give to have just listened to you and kept you home from that sleepover."

"So what happens now?" Lindsay's dad asked Officer Marshall.

"Lindsay will be given a court date that I will get for you before you leave. The judge will almost certainly require that she attend an alcohol-awareness class. I would recommend that Lindsay go ahead and do that now, before court. It will show the judge that she is concerned about what has happened and is becoming educated in the dangers and laws about alcohol. It can't hurt her, but it sure could help things. I can give you information about local groups who offer those classes before you leave tonight."

The officer left them to sit alone in the room while he gathered the information that he had offered to them. No one said a word in that small room. In the deafening silence, Lindsay felt as though the walls were closing in on her. All she wanted was for her mom to take her in her arms and hold her, promising that everything would be just fine—but Lindsay knew that she couldn't do that yet. So, she remained very alone in her regret and her fear.

The officer returned, had each of them sign a few papers, and gave them copies of everything they signed, as well as instructions for her court appearance—which was a full ninety days away.

Lindsay sighed. The uncertainty of this would be hanging over her head for at least that long.

The Martins were escorted to the door, and they left the station. At the car, Lindsay began to climb into the backseat and realized that she would never be able to get into the backseat of a car without remembering how it felt to be a common criminal on her way to jail. Nothing would ever be the same for Lindsay—or for any of them.

Chapter 10

CONSEQUENCES

The weeks that followed her arrest were even more difficult than Lindsay had imagined they could be. Not only had she been forced to face her parents' disappointment, but she'd also been the subject of whispers and secret conversations everywhere she went. At church, the youth council had a meeting about her and she was asked to step down from her new student-leader position in the youth group. At school, her teachers and guidance counselors no longer saw her as an exemplary student; she had become an example of a bad seed. In an attempt to make an example of her, she had even been suspended for three days. It seemed unfair that she was the only one who got suspended, but Lindsay didn't wish trouble on her friends—even though they did seem to be avoiding her.

She lived in constant fear and dread of the court date looming in the distance. Would she really have to spend time in jail or a juvenile facility? People told her that there was no way that it could happen for her first offense and for something so minor. But others, including her attorney, told her that her particular judge, rather than letting kids off easy, sometimes liked to make examples of young people as a deterrent for other kids.

She also had to attend the drug and alcohol meetings that Officer Marshall had recommended. Of all her punishments, those meetings were by far the worst. She sat there, twice each week, in the presence of adults who had real problems with drugs and alcohol—true addicts. Some of them were there as part of a probation deal, others were court ordered, and some were there voluntarily. But none of them were there as a thirteen-year-old girl who had tried to buy a beer, having never actually tasted alcohol in her life. She felt so conspicuously out of place, sure that no one understood why she was there at all.

Her parents agreed that it was a good idea for

her to attend the meetings because she could see firsthand how poor decisions caused big problems for people. She had to watch a video about people whose children were killed by drunk drivers. She learned about diseases and other horrible things that happened to drug users. It was a dark and very real glimpse at a world that Lindsay had never expected to see.

But far, far worse than any punishment or any meeting that she had to attend, Lindsay suffered under the crushing weight of her parents' disappointment. Every time she looked at them, she saw sadness in their eyes. She longed for the lighthearted days when happiness and trust filled her home. Lindsay knew that her parents blamed themselves, which made it even harder for her. She wished that it could be like when she was a little girl and did something wrong. The punishment was swift and just and then over. She wondered if the consequences of this mistake would ever end.

"Mom. . . " Lindsay hesitated as she walked into the family room where her mom was sitting and staring at a book whose pages she hadn't turned in over an hour.

"Yes, Lindsay, what is it?" her mom gazed up at her and tried to smile, but she still looked tired and sad.

Lindsay couldn't figure out what to say to get things back to the way they had been before. "Oh, nothing, Mom. Would you like for me to start dinner?"

"That would be nice, Lindsay. There's a box of frozen fried chicken in the freezer. You can just put that in the oven and make some macaroni and cheese. It'll be good to sit down and talk as a family over dinner."

Lindsay's heart sank. By *talk*, she knew that her mother meant Lindsay would have to listen to her parents tell her once again just how disappointed they were and how she would have to work hard to regain their trust.

She wanted to run, to hide, to pretend that everything was the same as it had been before the stupid dare. Instead she trudged into the kitchen to start dinner.

A month had gone by since that fateful night. Lindsay couldn't bear her parents' looks of disappointment any longer. Every time she was with them, she felt her guilt weighing heavily on her. She didn't want to carry it anymore, but she wasn't sure how to get rid of it. Lindsay felt like her parents only thought she was sorry because she had been caught. She just wasn't sure how to get them to see how truly sorry she was for what she did so that they would start believing in her again.

Then, Saturday afternoon during her quiet time, she read Proverbs 28:13: "He who conceals his sins does not prosper, but whoever confesses and renounces them finds mercy."

That's it! Lindsay had told her parents what she'd done, but she'd never confessed the sin behind it. She closed her Bible and stood up with purpose, resolved to finally put this to rest. Finding her mom upstairs folding laundry and her dad cleaning out the garage, Lindsay knew it was time to bring them together for a talk.

"Mom?" Lindsay called up the stairs.

"What, Lindsay?" Her mom called back.

"Can you come down here for a minute? I want to talk to you and Dad."

"I'll be right down."

When Lindsay heard that, she went to the garage door so she could call for her dad only to see that he was already on his way back into the house. "Oh good. I was just coming to get you. I'd like to talk to you and Mom, if you don't mind."

"Nothing has happened, has it?" Mr. Martin asked with a panicked tone.

"No, no, nothing like that. Just have a seat. Mom is on her way down."

When both of her parents were seated on the couch and looking at her with questioning eyes, Lindsay sat down in the chair opposite them but then jumped up again, nervous about how to say what she needed to say.

"Mom and Dad, I've asked for this opportunity to talk to you for several reasons. Mainly I want to tell you how sorry I am. I know I've said it before, but this is different. I'm not just sorry that I made a bad decision or that I got caught or even that I'm being punished—I deserve that, I know. I'm also just so very sorry because what I did wasn't just *wrong*; it was a *sin*." Lindsay sounded excited at the announcement of her realization.

Her parents looked at each other and then back at her, their faces not quite as stern as they'd been before. "Go on," her mom said.

"When Kelly told me what the dare was and if I didn't do it that I'd be kicked out of the group, I didn't really think about what it would mean to do it even though I knew it was wrong. I didn't think about how I would appear to the girls by willingly going along with something that my heart was telling me not to do."

Dad leaned forward, hands clasped together. "Why do you think your heart was telling you not to do it?"

"I think. . ." Lindsay swallowed hard, not sure exactly how to put her thoughts into words. "I think it was God telling me it was wrong. I think it was my conscience—the Holy Spirit— trying to show me that what I was about to do was a sin."

"But do you understand why it was a sin?" Mom asked, tears sparkling in her eyes.

"I think so. I think it's because by doing it, I wasn't being a good witness to the girls. I wasn't showing them that being a Christian means choosing to do things that are right, things that are good and holy, and choosing *not* to do things that are wrong—especially when they're illegal."

Lindsay ran out of steam and put her head in her hands and began to cry. A month of regret and fear had finally broken her. She was heartsick over the way she had ignored God's will and hurt her parents but so grateful for forgiveness and unconditional love.

Instantly her mom was at her side and her dad wasn't far behind. They held her and rocked her back and forth. Both of them were crying, too.

"Oh, Lindsay, sweetheart," her mom cried. "We have been praying so hard that you would finally come to understand this, that you'd understand we were still hurting. You hadn't asked God for forgiveness yet, and we couldn't force you to do it when you weren't ready."

"You've proven to us that you've learned from your mistake, Lindsay," her dad said, his voice gruff with emotion. "There is a difference between being sorry that you got into trouble and true repentance. We've been praying for you to find your way to true repentance." He paused for a moment. "Speaking of prayer, the one thing that I've missed most is that we haven't been praying together as a family since this happened."

"Yes!" Lindsay wiped at her tears. "I've missed praying with you guys so much! But I just couldn't do it because every time I thought about it, the guilt was so terrible that I couldn't breathe."

The three Martins joined hands. Lindsay felt an electric spark at the touch of her parents' hands. She realized that it had been almost a month since she had let either of them do that.

With a deep breath, her dad began, "Father, we come to You broken and sinful. Not one of us is perfect. We have all sinned and fallen short of Your goodness and grace. We need You now more than ever. Please fill us with Your peace, Your grace, Your wisdom. Thank You, Father, for answering our prayers and leading Lindsay back to You, back to her family. Unite us as a family once again."

"Jesus," Lindsay began to pray, "please, please forgive me for what I did. Help me to find forgiveness from those around me. Please show me how to rebuild the reputation that I have destroyed by my actions. And, Jesus, please help me to face my consequences and get through this time with my head held high. If You can use me in some way to reach other kids through this, please just show me how."

"Heavenly Father, I thank You for my family."
Mrs. Martin's voice caught as she began to cry
once again. "I thank You for my daughter, who
has found her strength in You and, like the little
lost lamb, has come back into the fold. Please
unite us, and help us get Lindsay through this
time. Lord, please let Lindsay know just how
much we love her. Show us how to help her and
give us wisdom to know what to do."

The Martins all said, "Amen," at the same
time, united once again.

Chapter 11

THE FREEDOM OF FORGIVENESS

"Morning, Mom," Lindsay said cheerfully, as she bounced into the kitchen. She looked refreshed and happy, like she'd had a great night's sleep. Mom smiled back at her daughter, reflecting the same sense of relief and buoyancy as Lindsay.

"What's gotten into you?" Mom teased.

"Oh nothing, really—I'm just relieved. Plus I have some work to do, and I'm anxious to get started on it."

"Work? What kind of work?" Lindsay's mom asked as she passed the milk so Lindsay could pour it over her cereal.

"Well, you and Dad and God aren't the only ones I need to fix things with. But I'm not really sure how to get started."

"You could start by talking with Pastor Steve. Tell him what you told us last night, and I know he'll be able to pray with you and maybe even give you a Bible study that will help you learn how to make better decisions in the future."

"That's a good idea. And I feel like I need to apologize to Sam's, Macy's, and Kelly's parents. They've always been so good to me, and I feel like I've really let them down."

"Maybe you could write each girl's parents a letter," her mom suggested. "I think that they all understand you weren't completely at fault, but taking responsibility for your actions will go a long way toward regaining their trust."

"Actually I think I'd rather talk to them— I want to ask for their forgiveness face-to-face so they can hopefully see that I mean what I say." Lindsay took a few bites of cereal. "Then I need to talk to the girls. I don't know if our friendship can ever be the same; after all, they did tell me that if I didn't do the dare, they wouldn't be my friends anymore. I can't just ignore that and pretend it didn't happen."

"I know you've been friends with them for a very long time, Lindsay," Mrs. Martin said, "but if they're going to put those kinds of conditions on your relationship, are you sure they're the right friends for you?"

Lindsay laid her spoon down on the table. "First I'll explain to them about why what I did was wrong—about how it was a sin and how I've confessed it to God and prayed for forgiveness. But then I'll explain that from now on I can only be friends with them as long as they don't pressure me to do things I know are wrong. If they can't agree to that, I'll have to tell them we can't hang out anymore. It'll hurt, but I know that I need to be strong and do what's right. So I'll do my best."

"Well, Linds, it sounds like you have a really full day ahead of you. I think it's a wonderful thing that you're doing. Do you want me to drive you?"

"No, thank you. I'd really rather take care of all this on my own. I mean, if that's okay. I know I'm grounded, but I promise I won't hang out or socialize."

"Lindsay, your dad and I feel that your punishment here at home has run its course. You've grown beyond what being grounded was teaching you. So, yes, I think it's fine and probably for the best that you go alone. I'll be praying for you the whole time, though." She reached across the table and hugged her daughter tightly.

Lindsay gave her mom a kiss, grabbed her bag, and left the house with a skip in her step. She was so happy to be back on the right track, and it showed in her every movement and on her face.

First stop: the church.

Lindsay hopped on her bicycle and headed in that direction. It took her almost thirty minutes to bike there, but it was a nice ride; the exercise and fresh air did her some good by clearing her mind and helping her prepare for her conversation with Pastor Steve. When she arrived at the church, she paused for a moment to take a drink of water from the water bottle in the holder on her bike. As she was standing there drinking her water, Pastor Steve pulled into the parking lot. He saw Lindsay and walked right up to her.

"Hey, Lindsay. How are you today?"

"I'm fine, Pastor Steve. I was hoping that we could have a chat. Do you have a few minutes?"

"Absolutely. Let me put my stuff down, and

I'll meet you in the youth center, okay?" Pastor Steve, wearing his usual blue jeans and polo shirt, took his brown gym bag and lunch bag into the church. When he came back through the parking lot, walking toward the youth center, Pastor Tim was with him.

"Lindsay," Steve began when he opened the door to the youth center, "do you mind if Pastor Tim joins us. . .or is there some reason that you'd like to speak privately?"

"No, actually that's great, because I was going to head into the church to talk with him when we got finished, so this works out great."

"So what's up?" The two pastors waited for her to collect her thoughts and begin.

"You probably know what I'm here for, and I'm sure you know all or most of the details about the events that happened. What I'd like to share goes back just a little bit before that, though." They nodded and remained silent, encouraging her to continue.

"Pastor Tim, about a month ago, before all of this happened, you preached a sermon about avoiding even the appearance of evil. And you explained about how sin creeps in and we aren't even aware of it until it's too late unless we're prepared for it."

"Well, at least I know that someone was listening." The pastor winked at her.

"Yeah, it really stuck with me. Actually, immediately after the sermon, before I left the church, I was able to put it into practice. I happened upon some kids who were messing around with cigarettes, and I realized that if I stayed with them and we were caught, even if I wasn't doing the bad behavior, I would be accused of it or at least of condoning it just by associating with them. Right?"

"Absolutely, Lindsay. That's exactly what I was talking about in my sermon."

"Well, look what happened to me. I guess I don't mean 'happened' to me, because it was my own doing. But it was a real live case of sin creeping in slowly and doing something that I didn't realize was so bad but has cost me a lot."

They both nodded their understanding, so Lindsay continued. "So, I guess what I'm here for is to ask for your forgiveness. I know that I disappointed both of you and deeply affected your trust in me even after you gave me a leadership role. I am just so sorry, and I hope that someday our relationship and trust can be restored."

"Lindsay," Pastor Steve jumped in, "we absolutely forgive you. Thank you for sharing with us. It's awesome to see such real understanding and application from someone your age. I am really proud of you. While I can't restore your leadership role just yet, it's still there and it's yours when the time is right. In the meantime, I wonder if you would be willing to share what you've told us with the youth group. Many young people would benefit from hearing your experiences and would hopefully apply them before they got into trouble. Would you do that?"

"I—I don't know if I'm quite ready to share yet with the whole youth group. I really need to work on straightening things out with my friends first, and I don't know how long that will take. But I might be able to share some of it eventually, even though it'll be really hard—I'll need to pray about it a lot to make sure my heart is really right with God before I do."

"Lindsay, my heart is so full of joy right now." Pastor Tim wiped his eyes. "I was grieved by what transpired, and I have prayed for you and your family nonstop since the beginning of all of this. I can see that my prayers have been answered mightily. You are an inspiration to me, young lady."

The pastors asked if they could pray with Lindsay before she left. During their prayer, Lindsay felt another piece to her puzzle of healing falling into place. She knew that another empty part of her had been filled by their forgiveness. As she rode her bike toward her neighborhood, she let the wind blow in her face—she felt so free.

One by one, Lindsay went to speak with the girls' moms, leaving Macy's mom for last. Kelly's mom was a little standoffish at first. But then she admitted that she admired Lindsay's strength and that she knew she hadn't acted alone. She said that she hoped the girls would be able to have the same old friendship back really soon but that it would be awhile before she would allow Kelly to attend a sleepover. Lindsay understood—she wasn't sure she wanted to go to a sleepover anytime soon, anyway. She didn't stay long—just long enough to make sure she said all she needed to.

At Sam's house, she was received much more warmly by Mrs. Lowell. "Oh, honey, you don't need to apologize to me. You sweet thing, you didn't do anything wrong. You didn't know."

"Mrs. Lowell, with all due respect, I did do many things wrong, and it's important that I own up to them. Whether or not I knew it was illegal, I knew in my heart it was wrong. Regardless of the involvement of the other girls, I want to take responsibility for my part. I feel the need to apologize to you for the bad example I was to Sam and for breaking your trust in me."

"Oh, you sweet thing. Don't give it another thought. Boy, your parents sure did things right with you. I'd like to know their secret."

"Their secret is easy: God is a daily part of our lives. They live the way they want me to live, and they uphold His high standards for me. That's all there is to it. Thanks a lot for your time, Mrs. Lowell. I have to be going now."

Sam's mom reached over and gave Lindsay a hug. "Say. . .if you can let any of that God stuff rub off you and onto Sam, I'd sure be appreciative."

"I'll do my best, Mrs. Lowell. I promise."

For the last stop on her road to forgiveness,

Lindsay pulled into the Monroes' driveway. Macy was sitting on the front porch by herself, looking sad and bored. When she saw Lindsay pull into the driveway, she perked up immediately. "Lindsay!" Macy ran to her and hugged her. "I know I see you in school, but it seems like so long since I've been able to really see you."

"I know, Mace. I miss you, too. It's been a long month. Unfortunately, I'm not here for social reasons today. I promised my parents that I would come and do what I needed to do and then head home. Things are getting a lot better, though. It won't be long until we can get caught up. I promise."

"Okay, Linds. So what are you here for, then?"

"I just need to talk to your mom, if she's around. You can come, too, if you want."

The girls walked into the cheery kitchen, where Mrs. Monroe was pouring hot coffee into a big mug. The dishwasher was running, and she had a magazine tucked under her arm.

"Mom, Lindsay is here to see you. She wants to talk to you."

"Well, hello there, Lindsay. Why don't you

two come out to the back porch with me? I just finished cleaning up the kitchen, and I was about to take my coffee outside. So it's perfect timing."

Mrs. Monroe sat on the white wicker glider that faced the chairs the girls sat in. "So, what's happening, Lindsay? What can I do for you?"

"Mrs. Monroe, I'll get right to the point, and I won't take up too much time. I am here to apologize to you for the things that I did and the bad influence I was on Macy. I really blew it, and the worst part is that you trusted me and expected me to have higher standards. So I wanted to apologize to you, especially." Lindsay went on to tell her of all the things that she had learned over the past month. By the time they were through talking, all three of them were crying.

"Lindsay, even in the midst of the worst trouble you have ever been in, you still manage to become an example that I want to hold up before Macy's eyes."

"Mrs. Monroe, the thing is, I am just like each of us. I am a human being who makes mistakes. But I am also forgiven by God. He offers that forgiveness to everyone and then calls us to a higher standard. It's perfectly all right to make mistakes, but it's not okay to keep making the same ones or to stay mired in them. Does that make sense?"

"Complete sense. I hope that you continue to grow into the young woman that you're becoming. And, please, don't be a stranger. We'd like to see you around here more. It's been awhile."

"Thanks, Mrs. Monroe, I appreciate it so much. I'll be back as soon as my parents start to feel more comfortable with me having more freedom. It'll just take some time."

They hugged and wiped their eyes. Macy walked Lindsay to her bike in the driveway, and Lindsay hopped on and started for home. She felt so free. She had done what she set out to do that day, and it felt great. There was just one more thing to do. . . .

"Hi, girls."

Lindsay was leaning against the big tree in front of the school when Macy, Kelly, and Sam got there the next morning. It was the first time since the last sleepover that Lindsay had joined them in the morning.

"Hi, stranger," Sam said. Macy just smiled.

Kelly stared at her for a minute. "I don't get why you've been hiding from us. I mean, are you angry with us?"

"I'll admit, Kelly, I was angry. But I'm over that. I had to get to the point where I was accepting responsibility for my own actions rather than blaming you guys. I was mad because I felt like I wasn't given the choice to not do the dare. I felt like my choice was to either just do it or lose your friendship. Like I said, I got over being mad because it was my choice, but I guess I felt like our friendship must not have meant as much to you if it was so easy for you to dispose of it when I didn't do what you said."

"Wow, I guess I can see how you would feel that way. We got carried away that night, didn't we?" Kelly asked.

Lindsay chuckled. "Yeah, I think that's safe to say. It's okay, though. I really am glad it happened. It brought my family closer together and closer to God. I now truly understand forgiveness. It's fine with me if you roll your eyes, Kell. It's just part of who I am. Can you accept me for me or not?"

"Of course I can, Lindsay. I'm so sorry that I pressured you and made you feel like you would lose our friendship."

"It's okay. It's not your fault that I did what I did. But if we are going to be friends, I just need to know that I can be myself 100 percent and not have to pretend I'm someone I'm not."

"It's a deal. Lindsay, I'm sorry."

"I'm sorry, too."

The four girls hugged each other for a long time. It felt so good to be back where they belonged—together. The bell rang, signaling the start of the school day, so the four girls walked together, arm in arm, up the stairs to the school. Lindsay watched their reflection in the front doors of the school. What she saw there were the same four girls whose reflections she had seen in that same door on the first day of school—only now they were wiser and stronger. Lindsay smiled at the thought of all they had been through and grinned even wider when she realized how far they had yet to go together. God was good.

My Decision

I, *(insert your name here)* Emily Kooy, have read the story of Lindsay Martin and have learned from the choices that she made and the consequences that she faced. I want to make choices that lead my life down the path that God has for me. I promise, from this moment on, to think before I act and, in all things, to choose God's will over mine. Specifically, I will honor my parents and avoid disobedience, even when I don't think my behavior is really wrong.

Please pray the following prayer:

Father God, I don't know everything, and I can't possibly have everything under control. Please help me remember the lessons I've learned as I've read this book. Help me to honor my parents and serve You by making right choices and avoiding questionable situations. It is my desire to be a witness to others about Your grace and love. I know I can't do that if my behavior is questionable. So if I get in a tight spot, please help me to find a way out and give me the strength to do what it takes. I know that You have everything under control, so I submit to Your will. Amen.

Congratulations on your decision! Please sign this contract signifying your commitment. Have someone you trust, like a parent or a pastor, witness your choice.

Emily Kooy
Signed

(signature)
Witnessed by *Mom*

ALL THAT GLITTERS

DEDICATION

This book is dedicated to my daughters, Natalie and Emily. Your sweet spirits and love for Jesus inspire me to live my own life of faith. I pray that this series of books will help you plan ahead and make commitments about the choices you will face. I'm so proud of you both, and I love you more than you could ever know.

—Mom

Chapter 1

TIME FOR A CHANGE

A fancy sports car on one side and a shiny, brand-new SUV on the other, Drew and Dani leaned forward eagerly as their mom slid her car into a parking spot at the mall. More than any other year, shopping for school clothes this year was a very important task. Dani and Drew, identical twins, were starting the ninth grade—the first year of high school. They knew full well how important their first impression was—well, at least Drew did. She had spent most of her summer planning and researching fashion trends, hairstyles, and makeup tips by reading fashion magazines. Not that it would do her much good, she often thought. Their parents didn't allow them to wear makeup; and her long, straight, dark hair looked just like her sister's and was cut and styled in the same style they had always had.

"Mom, I think it's time for a change," Drew announced as they walked through the parking lot toward the mall.

"What kind of change?" Mom asked hesitantly.

"You know, change isn't always a bad thing." Drew thought her mom might need some convincing. "Change can just be a part of growing up and a sign that a girl is secure and comfortable with herself."

"Yes, Drew, I'm aware of that. Why do I have a feeling that I'm not going to like what you're about to suggest?" Mom sighed goodnaturedly and looked at Drew's sister, who shrugged her shoulders, not knowing anything about the big change that her twin was proposing. "Well, let's have it. What have you got cooked up?"

"Oh, it's really not a big deal, Mom. I'd just like to get my hair cut." Drew pulled a picture of a hairstyle out of her pocket and showed it to her mom.

Even Mom had to admit that the softly layered style would cascade to a very flattering place just below Drew's shoulders. She looked at Dani and raised her eyebrows. "Do you want your hair cut like that?"

"No, Mom, you don't understand," Drew interrupted with a slight whine, nervous that she wasn't getting her point across. "If Dani cuts her hair like that, too, then I don't want to. This is how *I* want to look. . .by myself. I want to make a change, even just a slight one like my hairstyle, to separate myself from just being 'one of the twins.' I want to be an individual. I want to be Drew."

"Ah, I see, now." As the mother of twins, she had always known that this would happen one day and, she had to admit, high school was a reasonable time for it to occur. It pained her to think of her baby girls reaching such an independent place, though. "How do you feel about that, Dani?"

"Well, to be honest, I really don't want to change my hair. And I like being 'one of the twins', as Drew put it. I guess I don't see how that's a bad thing. Why would changing your hair to look like a picture of someone else make you an individual anyway?" she asked pointedly, turning to Drew.

"It just gives me the chance to express myself and be different than I have been."

"As long as you really mean 'different than you have been' and not just that you want to be different than me." Dani sounded hurt.

"Aw, sis, I love you. Nothing can change that we're twins. That will always be a part of us. We're just talking about a haircut here."

"I guess you're right." Dani laughed. "Let's go get your hair cut so we can all get used to it while we try on clothes."

First stop: Shear Expressions for a new hairstyle. Luckily, there was no one ahead of her, because Drew was too excited and impatient to wait. She took her seat in the shampoo chair, and the stylist began to lather up her hair. After the shampooing was finished, she patted Drew's head dry and moved her to the station where she would be cutting her hair.

Drew struggled to get her hand into the front pocket of her jeans so she could show the stylist the picture of the haircut that she wanted. "Um, Drew, I didn't realize that your jeans were getting so tight. We're going to have to be sure to buy some new jeans today."

"*Mom*." Drew laughed. "This is how I bought them. I want them this way."

Mrs. Daniels looked at the stylist, obviously

a mom herself, and shrugged her shoulders. "I know," the stylist said, "it looks uncomfortable to me, too."

"This is what I want." Drew showed her the picture, ignoring the comments about her jeans.

"Oh, that's going to be easy enough and beautiful, too. We'll just take this hair of yours and cut some layers into it. We'll probably need to take off about three inches, but you have plenty of length, so it won't even be that noticeable. Are you doing the same cut?" The stylist turned to Dani.

"Nope, not me. I'm staying just like this."

"All right then, let's get started."

Thirty minutes later, with dark hair in little piles all over the floor around her, Drew was staring into the mirror in front of her, getting her first look at her new self. She was stunned by what she saw. After looking at her sister for so many years, she was used to having a walking mirror right beside her. But now, as they both gazed into the mirror and took in the changes, they realized that a simple thing like a haircut signaled major changes afoot. Dani was sad when she saw the differences between them, but Drew was thrilled with her new look.

"I *love* it!" She spun around to the right and then to the left and watched her hair bounce in waves around her shoulders. "It moves, and it's free." She didn't miss the long, thick straight locks a bit. "It has personality. Thank you so much. You did a perfect job," she said to the hairdresser.

"I'm so glad you like it. I think it looks great, too." Both the hairdresser and Mrs. Daniels were a bit more reserved out of sensitivity to Dani.

"Mom, what about you? Do you like it?"

"You look beautiful, dear. Very grown-up."

"Now I'm ready to shop." Nothing was going to contain Drew's excitement as they left the salon; she was thrilled.

"We need to be wise now, girls. There is a limit to today's budget. My question is whether you want to split the money and each get your own clothes—or do you want to pick things out to share and get more that way?"

Drew was trying to be more of an individual, but even she could see the logic behind pooling their resources and sharing the clothing allowance; and she knew that Dani would agree. But Drew did have one trick up her sleeve that she decided to save for later in the day.

They spent the day trying on clothes. It helped that both girls were exactly the same size and basically liked similar things. By the end of the day, they had successfully managed to supply their wardrobe with all of the basics they would need for ninth grade, including new winter jackets, jeans, tops, sweaters, belts, socks, pajamas, undergarments, accessories, and shoes. They were exhausted by the end of the shopping trip, and Mom was more than ready to leave.

As they were walking toward the exit door, Drew said, "Mom, you mentioned that you have grocery shopping to do. Would it be all right if Dani and I stay here and meet up with you when you're finished? I have a few things I still want to look for."

"I suppose that would be okay, but I'm done with dishing out money today. So what are you looking for, and what will you do once you find it?" Mom laughed.

"I brought some of the money I saved from babysitting this summer, and I really want to use some of it to get a few unique shirts or something that will be just mine—you know, signature pieces. I promise I won't spend it all."

"Oh, I see. This is part of your search for

individuality? Is that it?" At Drew's nod, she continued, "I don't see anything wrong with that. But, Drew, just remember what your dad and I allow and how we expect you to dress. No supertight jeans, no shirts that show your belly, nothing with a saying or advertisement that your dad and I would find inappropriate. Think of it this way: nothing that I wouldn't let you wear to youth group. Deal?"

"Got it, Mom. Thanks, you're the best."

After they discussed their meeting time and location, Mom left the girls to their shopping. Dani wasn't too happy about it, though. "Why couldn't you have done this while we were shopping earlier?"

"Because I wanted to finish the shopping for our stuff, and then I would know what I still needed."

"Oh, sis, there's nothing else that you *need*."

"I know, that's what makes this part so fun. It's all about what I *want*."

Dani sighed and suggested they get started before they ran out of time. With her own money, Drew selected two snug plaid shirts to wear over a tight black T-shirt that she found. The flannel shirts barely reached her waistband, but the T-shirt was long enough, so she thought it would pass. She also selected a cropped denim jacket that was covered in studded rhinestones. Dani liked the jacket, but it wasn't really her style at all. Drew also picked a few cropped sweaters that, if worn alone, would be way too short for her mom's approval, but with a T-shirt or tank underneath, would probably get by. Her favorite and most expensive purchase was a black leather belt with a big silver buckle covered in rhinestones in the shape of a big rose. Her signature piece.

"Well, one thing you won't have to worry about," Dani assured her, "is me bugging you to borrow any of the things you bought. They're all yours."

Their time was up so they hurried to the exit door to find Mrs. Daniels already waiting there for them. As they slipped into the car, she asked, "Well, was your search successful?"

"Oh, yeah! I found some really cute things."

"Yeah, real cute," Dani said, rolling her eyes.

Mom raised her eyebrows and said, "Great. Then we can have our own private fashion show when we get home."

"Sure, Mom. No problem."

After dinner, Mom sat on the couch. "Drew, why don't you get those things that you bought so we can make sure that everything is acceptable for you to wear."

"Mom, I know the rules and I followed them. I don't see what the concern is."

"There's no real concern, honey, but I'd appreciate if you don't argue with me and just humor me. I am only looking out for your best interests."

"Okay, okay, I'll go get them." Drew left to get her bags from the room that she shared with her sister. She stomped down the hall, careful not to be disrespectful, but made sure that her mom knew she wasn't happy.

Plopping her bags down on the couch, Drew waited for the verdict. Her mom wasn't too happy at all when she saw how small and short some of the shirts were. Drew said, "Hold on, Mom. Before you say no, let me try them on."

Skeptically, she agreed to reserve judgment until she had a chance to see the items on Drew.

After Drew had the first outfit on, Mrs. Daniels realized that they were layering pieces and that the shorter items were worn on top to reveal the layers beneath. "Well, now, that's not so bad. But, Drew, you have to promise me that I'm not going to catch you wearing those clothes alone or in any way that shows your belly."

"I already know that, Mom."

She raised her eyebrows, waiting.

"Okay, I promise. Really."

"Well, then, everything is fine; and I especially like the belt you bought. It's definitely a cool piece."

Dani had been sitting quietly on the other side of the room, watching the process and waiting for the verdict. She quietly got up and went to her room, softly closed the door, and got ready for bed. She wasn't too happy, but she didn't really know what it was that was bugging her.

"Too many changes," she whispered as she drifted off to sleep.

Chapter 2

MAKING A MARK

They woke to the sound of steady rain on their windows. Because of the weather, the girls decided to ride the bus to school that day even though they much preferred to walk. Nervously, they waited on the porch and watched the corner at the end of their street for the first sign of the big yellow bus as it turned onto their street.

The bus slowed to a stop in front of their house while Dani and Drew scrambled to gather up their backpacks and purses from their perch on the front porch. Squeezing between the familiar seats, the girls stepped over the legs that spread far into the aisle and the backpacks carelessly strewn across the seat backs as they searched for an open seat to share. They headed toward the back of the bus but stopped short of the last few rows, knowing that those were reserved for the seniors. Ninth graders had to sit somewhere in the middle of the bus, and if they attempted to sit somewhere else, the seniors would make sure they paid for it. They chose a seat and settled in for the short ride.

As the bus pulled away from their house, Drew pulled out a small bag and unzipped it. Dani looked on with interest. "What's in the bag?"

Drew grinned wickedly and pulled out a tube of lipstick and waved it in Dani's face. "Look what I've got."

Drew had managed to smuggle a full set of makeup and a mirror out of the house without being seen. Dani just watched as Drew applied the makeup that she hoped would make her look even older than a ninth grader.

At Drew's insistent prodding, Dani applied some sheer lip gloss and just a tiny bit of sparkly blue eye shadow to her fresh face. She liked what she saw in the mirror and handed it over to Drew, who shook her head.

"That's all you're going to put on?" she taunted Dani. "This is your chance. Are you chicken?"

Dani wouldn't take the bait—she felt guilty enough already—so Drew gave up with a shrug of her shoulders and continued to cake it on.

First, she applied some heavy black eyeliner around her eyes and then mascara to her lashes. The bumpy bus ride made the mascara difficult to apply, but eventually she managed. Then Drew took out the red lipstick and began to apply it to her full lips.

Dani gasped. "Do you have any idea what you look like?"

"I don't care," Drew replied. "I like it."

Shaking her head, Dani allowed Drew to continue; but, wanting no part of the mess, she took out a book and pretended to read while watching Drew out of the corner of her eye.

The bus slowly squealed to a stop in front of the school. The girls stood from their seats—the sticky plastic peeled from the backs of their legs leaving red, sweaty marks—and collected their things.

"Hold on," Drew said as she grabbed Dani's sleeve. "Let's let everyone else pass, and then we'll get off." The girls waited, and when the last student passed them to get off the bus, they began to make their exit. As they stepped out into the aisle, Drew paused for a second and rolled her gray plaid knit skirt up a few inches. The skirt that had once reached Drew's knees, and the skirt that her mother was thrilled to see Drew wearing to the first day of school, became a miniskirt that Drew would never have been allowed to wear out of the house. She looked like a completely different person than the one who had kissed her mom as she left the house this morning—a person Dani wasn't sure she liked.

"What are you hoping to accomplish with this new look of yours?" Dani asked her sister, making no attempt to hide her disgust as she looked from her heavily made-up face to her now-revealed knees.

"What do I hope to accomplish? Well, sis, I intend to have a boyfriend this year; and I want to be noticed for me, not just for being one of a pair. It's time to make my mark on this school. It's time to shine." Drew lifted her chin triumphantly.

"Well, don't bump into anyone—or with all of that makeup on your face, you'll make your mark all over their shirt," Dani replied sarcastically.

"Don't be jealous, sweet sis. You, too, can have all of this and more." Drew made an exaggerated flourish as she moved toward the front of the bus as she stopped to look in the driver's rearview mirror long enough to fluff her new haircut and check her teeth for any lipstick smears. Satisfied, she smiled at her reflection, while Dani just rolled her eyes.

Exiting the bus, the girls entered the throng of students making their way toward the front door of the school. Smiling, Drew sneaked up on several of their friends. When they turned to see who was behind them, they all registered shock at Drew's appearance.

"Oh my goodness! You sure changed a lot over the summer. I really love your hair," Cara shouted above the noisy crowd.

"You look like a different person," Stacey said in shock.

"Did your mom let you dress like that?" Cara wondered.

"You two don't look anything alike anymore. I'll have no problem telling you apart now."

Dani was stopped short by this last comment. Suddenly she wasn't feeling so well and just wanted to escape the crowd. Mumbling something about making it to her homeroom class on time, she darted away, getting lost in the crowd before her sister even noticed that she was gone.

But Drew was too enthralled with the attention she was getting to pay much notice. Before entering the school, Drew pulled out her pocket mirror and reapplied her lipstick, as her fresh-faced friends looked on in awe.

Crash! While Drew was looking in the mirror, something crashed hard into her back and sent her sprawling in the grass. Dazed, she sat there for a moment trying to compose herself and then looked around to see if she could find her backpack and purse that went flying. Her mirror lay broken on the sidewalk, and her lipstick was rolling away, headed under the bus.

"Oh, man, I am so sorry."

Drew looked up to see the cutest boy in school standing over her head, offering her a hand to help her up. As she allowed herself to be righted, she looked at the boy. It was Trevor Jaymes, the captain of the varsity football team and star quarterback, in his clean, game-day uniform. Once he had her standing upright, he took off to find her things. Drew and her friends just watched as he picked up the pieces of her mirror and ran off to catch the still-rolling lipstick.

Drew couldn't help but giggle when Trevor walked toward her, trying to figure out how to twist the lipstick back down so he could put the lid on it. He pushed on it for a minute and quickly realized that wouldn't work. He looked perplexed when he saw the red smudges on his fingers. Looking for somewhere to wipe his hands, he shrugged and wiped them on his white football pants, which caused pink streaks.

As she watched Trevor struggle with the lipstick, Drew couldn't contain herself any longer, so she began to laugh. Then, Trevor, determined to get that lipstick to close, pressed hard on the lid and then realized that he completely smashed the top of the stick.

"I am so sorry for everything," Trevor said as he walked toward her, appearing to blush with each step. "I think I wrecked your stuff." With a red face, he held out the broken pieces of Drew's mirror and her ruined tube of lipstick.

Drew couldn't help but laugh at his discomfort. "It's no big deal," she assured him. "It's really nothing." She noticed that he was giving her a funny look and standing there a little longer than he needed to. He was so cute—the cutest boy in school, really. She was sure that he would never be interested in a freshman like her. He was a junior, after all. She was lucky he even stopped to talk to her.

"What's your name anyway?" Trevor asked her as he was backing away from the group.

"It's Drew," she answered him, coyly not offering any further information.

"I'm Trevor Jaymes," he shot back as he got farther away.

"Oh, I know who you are," Drew answered and then began to blush as she realized that she shouldn't have said that; she should have played it a little cooler. In order to redeem herself, she turned away before he did and flipped her long, dark hair back over her shoulders as she started to walk away, making sure her waves bounced as she walked.

"Catch you later, Drew," he called after her. Proud of herself, Drew pretended not to hear him and continued to walk away.

"Why didn't you answer him? He clearly liked you." Stacey was appalled that Drew had been rude to Trevor.

"Oh, Stacey, you have a lot to learn about boys." Drew laughed. "You never want to be too eager, and you always want to keep them guessing. They will never want what comes easily to them. If you play hard-to-get, it will make you look more important."

"How did you get so smart? You've never even had a boyfriend," Cara pointed out.

"While Dani was reading the actual Bible, I read *Seventeen* magazine all summer. It's the bible of boys and fashion. You girls should check it out." She pointedly looked them up and down and then laughed, teasing them.

On her way to class, Drew stopped in the hallway to check out the notice board. Her friends paused with her, curious to see what she was looking for. Nodding her head, Drew turned away from the wall, looking satisfied at her find.

"What?" Cara asked. "You're so full of mystery these days. What did you see there that you liked?"

"I think I'm going to try out for the cheerleading squad, and I wanted to find out when tryouts are. That's all," Drew answered.

"Oh, I think you should," Stacey encouraged. "What does Dani think?"

"Well, that's the thing. I'd like her to do it, too. But it hardly seems to be her thing, you know?"

"Speak of the. . .well. . .angel, here she is," Cara said as Dani turned the corner and joined the group.

"Who's the angel?" Dani laughed.

"So, you and Drew are going to go out for the cheerleading squad, I hear." Stacey baited her. Drew shot daggers at Stacey with a glare that even Dani didn't miss.

"I told them you hadn't decided yet."

"Hadn't decided *yet*? The words 'cheerleading squad' have never even been spoken to me. I had no idea this was something I was supposed to be deciding."

"I was just thinking that it would be something fun for us to do together." Their friends slowly backed away and headed off in different directions, sure there would be an argument.

"No, you're more interested in things that you can do alone these days. It doesn't matter anyway; I am not trying out for cheerleading, and you already know that." Dani was emphatic in her answer—it was not something she wanted to do then, or ever.

"Come on, sis, you might enjoy it." Drew gave a halfhearted attempt at coaxing Dani, but she secretly hoped to be able to do it alone. "I'm not trying to find things to do that you aren't interested in. . .I'm just trying to explore other options, you know, spread my wings a bit."

"Well, I suppose you have the right to do things, just as I have the right not to do things." Dani sighed, resigned to the fact that she and her sister were pulling apart. It was inevitable, she supposed.

The bell rang, and it was time to go to class. Not wanting to end the conversation on a sad note, Drew gave her sister a hug and promised that everything would be fine. "Oh, you know me, Dan. It's probably just a phase I'm going through. Just let me try some things out and test the waters a little bit. I'll probably realize that I liked it better the other way."

"Yep, knowing you, that's true." Both girls laughed and headed off to their classes.

Chapter 3

GIVE ME A "YES"

"Girls, I need you all to line up. We're going to teach you a cheer and then have you perform it. What we are looking for is style, smile, and choreography." The cheerleading coach, Tracy, was leading the after-school tryouts out on the football field on Friday afternoon. "If you get tapped on the shoulder, it means that we're asking you to step out of the tryouts. Please understand that we appreciate your efforts, but there are only seven freshman positions available for the junior varsity squad and about thirty girls who are trying out for them. At this time, though, I'm going to turn things over to our head cheerleader, Kallie, who will teach you the routine. Good luck, girls."

The coach sat on a chair on the sidelines with

a clipboard poised on her lap for note- taking. The thirty hopefuls who were trying out for the squad lined up on the field awaiting their instructions. Drew looked up and down the two rows of girls, sizing up her competition. She knew at least two of the girls had prior dance experience and three others had been in gymnastics with Drew. She wasn't sure about the dancers, but she knew that she was more skilled than the other gymnasts. She also noticed that there were many girls who weren't really contenders for a spot for various other reasons. As she waited, she began to grow a bit more confident that she could secure one of the spots on the team.

Kallie took her position in front of the girls, and two of her cheerleaders joined her and flanked her, one on each side. She began to teach the girls the cheer that they would have to learn for their audition. First, Kallie and the other two cheerleaders performed the cheer three times for the girls to watch. One thing that Drew took note of was that they smiled the entire time, even while they were shouting the cheer. After they had the chance to watch it three times, Kallie took them through the moves and the words one section at a time. It was unnerving to see that

Tracy, the coach, had begun to move about the rows of girls, looking at them closely as they practiced. A few times, she tapped girls on the shoulder to let them know that they were excused from the tryouts. That just made Drew work even harder at keeping that smile on her face and getting the moves just right.

After almost two hours of practicing, they were almost ready to perform the cheer as their final audition for Coach Tracy, who had left the field about an hour earlier. Before she went off to find the coach, Kallie asked, "Is there anyone who can do a back flip and would feel comfortable performing it for your audition? Since you have all done so well, I have a little surprise in mind for Tracy."

Three girls raised their hands, including Drew. Kallie gave each of them a chance to show her their back flip so she could select one girl to perform it for Tracy in the audition. First was Delaney. She was a decent gymnast and, if she nailed it, she could possibly be the best one to perform the flip, but she was often inconsistent, as Drew knew from gymnastics practice and meets. So Drew was anxious to see how she did. Delaney stood back and set off on a little run, did a round-off, and then a back flip. Her moves were fine, but she stumbled at the end rather than standing tall and solid. Her stumble caused her to lose her concentration, so her smile wavered.

Drew didn't know the second girl but was glad to see that her back flip was nowhere near as good as Delaney's was. It was Drew's turn. She wanted to nail this so badly. She looked down the line of girls who were waiting to see how she'd perform. She put a big smile on her face and set off on her run, preparing for her flip. She, too, did a round-off first and then a flip. It was perfect! She ended without a wobble and raised her arms as high as she could with a big smile on her face the entire time.

Kallie announced that Drew would be performing the trick at the end of their audition. They ran through the cheer one more time, adding in the specialty move that would be a surprise to Tracy.

After seeing the finished product, before she called Tracy back to view the final audition, Kallie told the girls her thoughts. "I am so surprised and impressed with this freshman group. You have done a fantastic job, and it's going to be a very difficult choice for us to make. I wish you all the best of luck." With that, she went to find Tracy, leaving the girls to take a break while she was gone.

"Okay, girls, let's see what you've got." Tracy came back, eager to see what the girls had learned and more than ready to begin the selection process for the new junior varsity cheerleading squad.

"Ready? Begin," Kallie shouted, calling for the cheer to start. The girls waited the two seconds they were supposed to and then began. The cheer went remarkably well except for a few girls who forgot the words and a few others who missed their cues. They were out of the running. At the end of the cheer, Drew poised herself to perform her big finish. It went perfectly, even better than the first time. She was exhilarated and proud when the cheer was over and they all turned to look at Tracy.

"I must say, girls, I am very impressed. You went above and beyond what was called for and even added difficulty to the routine. This is going to be a difficult selection process. You can look at the bulletin board outside of the sports office for the results on Monday morning."

Drew left the tryouts excited and hopeful, but

as she walked home, she became worried. It was sure to be a long weekend while Drew anxiously awaited the results of her cheerleading tryouts.

"Of course you'll make the squad. You got to do the big finish that impressed the coach," Dani tried to assure her numerous times. Drew even showed Dani the cheer to get her opinion. "You look like a natural-born cheerleader, Drew. Stop worrying about it." Dani was so irritated by the end of the weekend that she couldn't wait to get the results on Monday morning either, just so the constant talking about it would be over.

Monday morning couldn't have come soon enough for Drew. She jumped out of bed as soon as the alarm began to ring instead of pushing the SNOOZE button three times like she usually did. She yanked on the window shades, which opened with a loud *snap* and flapped as they rolled up. Bright sunlight streamed through the windows and filled the pretty, pink room. Dani began to stir and then groaned as she tried to open her eyes to the bright light.

"What are you doing?" Dani whined, rubbing her eyes. "We have more time to sleep. Why are you torturing me?"

"Dani! You need to get up right away. We have to leave for school as soon as we can get ready." Drew was so excited, she could barely contain it.

"Is this because of the cheerleading list?" Dani asked with obvious irritation.

"Of course. I've been waiting all weekend to see the results. Now come on." Drew pulled on the floral quilt that Dani held up by her chin.

"Okay, okay, I'm getting up. Give me a second."

"I'm going to use the bathroom. Please, please, please don't go back to sleep," Drew begged.

After Drew prodded Dani through breakfast and hurried her into dressing and packing her backpack, they loaded in the car and waited for their mom. She had agreed to drive them so Drew wouldn't have to wait for the bus or walk. "Come on, Mom," Drew called through the open window.

"I'm coming. Hold your horses," Mom climbed into the car.

As soon as they got to school, Drew said a hurried good-bye to her mom and Dani and then jumped out of the car and sprinted toward the building. Dani quietly watched her go, shaking her head with a smile and wondering how they could be identical twins, yet so incredibly different.

Drew ran right to the sports office and stared at the bulletin board, so anxious to see the list of the new squad members but afraid at the same time that she hadn't made it. Going down the list of names. . ."Stephanie Akers, Melanie Coldwell, Emily Frankle. . ." A lump caught in Drew's throat as she realized that the alphabetical list of the names of the girls who had been selected to be a part of the JV squad, the varsity squad, and the dance team didn't include her name. She hadn't made the team.

Not knowing what to think and not wanting to face anyone for fear of bursting into tears, Drew just stood there staring at the list. She was so disappointed and, admittedly, surprised. Continuing down the list, she read the names and sighed as she neared the bottom.

Still having trouble dealing with the news, she decided to read the list again. Starting at the top, she made her way to the bottom. Her name never magically appeared among the other girls' names. As she was about to give up and step away, she stopped short as she noticed her name at the bottom of the page, separate from the list.

She stepped a little closer and read the note in italics: *"Drew Daniels; Junior Varsity Cheerleading Squad Captain."*

So she had made the team! And not only had she made the team, but she was given the high honor of being the team captain. Her heart was beating wildly in her excitement.

"Drew, welcome to the team." Coach Tracy walked up behind her and patted her on the back.

"Thank you so much, Coach. I didn't see my name at first, and I panicked a little. I wanted this so badly, and I appreciate the extra responsibility you've given me by making me team captain. I didn't even know that was a possibility for a freshman."

"Well, Drew, your tryouts were exceptional; you definitely stood out among your peers, and you went above and beyond what the rest of the girls did. I also spoke with a few of your teachers from last year. It seems that you have a reputation for being a kind and fair leader in school. So it was a logical choice. I'm sure you'll do very well."

"Thanks for the vote of confidence, Coach," Drew said. "I promise I won't let you down."

It was an exciting day for Drew. Her new position on the cheerleading squad and her role as captain gave her instant celebrity among the freshman class.

Dani, on the other hand, plodded through her day with growing resentment of Drew's new focus and popularity. She didn't want to be jealous, and it wasn't exactly jealousy that she felt. She just felt left out. Dani and Drew had been inseparable, a single unit, for their whole lives up until this first week of school. All of a sudden everything changed and she was left standing alone, and Drew didn't even seem to notice. It seemed like Drew wanted to be as far from her as possible and didn't even seem to miss her and the tight bond they had, while Dani felt like a part of her had died.

Everywhere she went that day, people were saying things like, "Drew is the captain of the cheerleaders—isn't that fabulous? She's going to look so cute in the uniform." Or, "Why didn't you try out for the squad, Dani? I'm sure you'd have made it like Drew did." Or, "What are you going to do with all of your time now that Drew will be so busy with practices and games? I'll bet she'll make a lot of new friends, too." Each comment was like a knife through her heart. By the end of the day, all she wanted was to be home, in her room, alone.

Chapter 4

SQUEAKY CLEAN

Two days later, on the bus ride home, Drew was still unrelenting with her annoying chatter about her news. She wanted to talk about her schedule, her uniform, her practices, her leadership goals, her future plans—it was like this one moment, this one thing, had redefined her life.

"You know, Drew, I seriously think you need to settle down. I'm happy for you and all, but you're taking it a little too far, don't you think?" Dani had reached her limit.

After looking at her for a moment, Drew asked, "What has gotten into you lately? You have been so glum this whole week and you've hardly said a word all day." After Dani remained silent for a few seconds, Drew said, "Ah, I get it. You're jealous. Don't forget, I tried to get you to try out, too."

"Drew, I'm not jealous. . .I'm. . .oh, forget it, you'll never understand if you haven't figured it out already."

At that moment, the bus pulled up in front of their house and the doors squeaked open to let them off. Once in the house, Drew wanted to finish their talk, so she started to ask Dani more questions, but Dani held up her hand to stop her. "Let's just let it go for now. I would like to salvage part of this day. We have a couple of hours until youth group tonight, so let's do something together."

"That's a good idea, but first I have to call Stephanie. She said she has some big news for me. I think Trevor asked her about me or something. When I'm done, we can do our nails or watch TV or something."

"Oh never mind, I'll just do my homework," Dani answered, not wanting to be second choice to Drew's other, newer friends.

"Suit yourself," Drew replied cheerfully as she grabbed the phone and headed up the stairs to their bedroom. Dani settled on the couch to do her homework and watch some TV. They only had an hour until their mom was due home anyway. They would have dinner and then go to church. Tonight was supposed to be a special night at youth group, and Dani had been looking forward to it. Pastor Steve had cooked up a surprise for them, so she didn't know what would be happening. She hoped it would be really good; she needed the diversion.

The minutes ticked by, and it was ten minutes to five before Dani even realized it. Drew was still upstairs on the phone, but Dani was finished with today's homework and had gotten a start on some that wasn't due until later in the week.

Finally, Drew came back downstairs and replaced the phone in its cradle on the wall. "I wonder what Mom's planning for dinner tonight," Drew said, looking for clues in the refrigerator. At just that moment, Drew stopped in her tracks when she heard the garage door begin to open. "Oh no." She gasped. "Stall Mom. I haven't washed off my makeup yet." She ran up the stairs to the bathroom where she slammed the door.

Mom came in, arms laden with grocery bags. "Girls, I could use a hand here," she called, cheerfully summoning the girls to come help her unload and put away the groceries.

"I'll help you, Mom," Dani offered, immediately getting off the couch.

"Great, where's Drew?" Mrs. Daniels asked as Dani started to unpack the plastic grocery bags.

"Last I heard she was in the bathroom. She should be right down," Dani answered, being very careful not to lie.

"How was your day, sweetie?"

"Oh, it was okay. Nothing special to report from me. . . ." Dani smiled and held up her hand to fend off what she knew was going to be her Mom's next question. "And don't ask. I'm sure Drew'll want to fill you in about her day herself." Dani giggled when her mom closed her mouth. It was clear that she was about to ask about Drew's day, but Dani was tired of talking about her. She hurriedly put away the groceries so she could excuse herself from the kitchen before Drew came down. The last thing she wanted was to have to endure yet another conversation having anything to do with cheerleading.

"I'm done, Mom. I'll be upstairs if you need me." She breezed through the doorway just as Drew, freshly scrubbed, came into the kitchen.

"Hi, Mom. Guess what?"

Dani hurried up the stairs so that she didn't have to hear what Drew was about to say.

In the kitchen, Mrs. Daniels listened to Drew recount the details of her day. Drew was bubbling over with excitement about her newfound popularity.

"Sweetheart, I'm so proud of you. I think it's fantastic that you made the team and even better that you were selected to be a leader. What a great honor. Like I've been saying, that sort of thing looks wonderful on college applications too. But. . ."

"I know, Mom. It's really exciting," Drew interrupted. "Nothing like this has ever happened to me. It's weird doing it without Dani, though. But it's probably for the best," Drew explained. "We can't do everything together forever."

"Well, sweetie, just be careful that you don't leave your sister behind and make her take a backseat to your new interests. She's your sister; she's your best friend. She will always be a part of your life. Other friends, teams, interests. . .they will all come and go. But Dani will be the one person who will always be by your side. Just don't leave her in your dust as you pursue this new independence that you seem to want so badly."

"I'm not being insensitive, am I, Mom? I don't want to hurt her. I'm really not trying to."

"I know you're not trying to hurt her. But sometimes people get hurt even with the best of intentions. Think back over the past week. Have you even asked her anything about her life or have you just spent the last few days talking about yourself? Show some interest in her, and let her know that you haven't completely changed and that she is still just as important to you as she was before all of these changes started."

"Oh no, Mom. . ." Drew's face fell when she remembered. "Dani asked me to do something with her this afternoon and I told her I had to call Stephanie first. I stayed on the phone until just about the time you came home." Drew left out the part about needing to scrub the makeup off her face before her mom saw her.

"That's the kind of thing I'm talking about. By doing that, Drew, you basically told her that she wasn't as important as your new friends. I know that you don't feel that way, but you have to think about how Dani might feel. Do you understand what I mean?"

"Yeah, Mom, I get what you're saying. I'll be

more careful and try to be more thoughtful."

"That's all you can do, sweetie. Now I'm going to heat up dinner. You girls get ready for church. We need to leave in about forty-five minutes, and your dad should be home in fifteen minutes. So we'll sneak dinner in before we leave."

"Sounds good." Drew took off up the stairs planning on getting changed for church but also hoping to patch things up with Dani.

Arriving at church with barely enough time to get to their groups, Mr. and Mrs. Daniels headed off to their adult Bible study class while Dani and Drew went to youth group in the building behind the church. It had once been a parsonage before the church was completely rebuilt and updated. At that time, the old house was given to the youth group and converted into an activity center. It had couches and chairs, a big screen TV for watching movies, some game tables, a foosball table and pool table, as well as a kitchen stocked with basics and cooking equipment. It was a great place to hang out.

Tonight there was something special going on. The girls had been speculating on the drive over as to what it could be. Drew thought it was probably a pizza party, but Dani didn't think that was special enough to warrant all the hush-hush and surprise talk. Dani thought there was probably a special guest due to be there. But she had no idea who it could be.

With no fanfare or introduction, the doors opened and in walked three players from the Pittsburgh Steelers football team and two of their cheerleaders—all dressed in uniform. Drew was immediately enthralled and stared with her mouth open for at least a full minute. She finally got over her shock and looked at Dani in excitement.

Dani sat quietly, shaking her head, thinking her day couldn't possibly get any worse. She had definitely had enough of anything to do with cheerleading for a very long time; and she certainly never expected to have to face it at church, too. But it looked like she was going to have to deal with it for at least another couple of hours.

One of the players went to the front of the group and introduced himself for those who didn't know who he was. "Hi, everyone. I'm Shane Sutter. I'm one of the quarterbacks from the Pittsburgh Steelers. You're all probably

wondering why we're here with you today."
When everyone excitedly acknowledged his
introduction and nodded in agreement, Shane
continued. "Well, the five of us have a special
calling or a special desire, you might say, to
work with teens. We have all had very different
experiences, but the one thing that we share in
common is that our different roads have led us
to a point where we realized that we could do
nothing without Jesus. Tonight we'd each like
to share a little bit about our pasts and how we
came to know Jesus, and then we'll give you
guys a chance to ask us questions. We're pretty
informal so just relax, grab a drink or a snack,
and let's get started."

No one moved to get a snack. They were all
too excited to hear what their celebrities had to
say. One by one, the athletes shared their testimonies with the teens. A common thread
through the stories was the poor decisions that
they made that led to rough patches in their
lives. Shane told the story of a time when he
was playing football in college and he got the
surprise of his life when his girlfriend got preg-
nant. He recounted the fears and doubts of
sticking by her side through the pregnancy and

then the agonizing reality of giving the baby up for adoption.

"One thing I learned through that whole experience, something I still carry with me today, is that my choices are never just about me. Other lives are affected by what I do. I have to be willing to live with seeing the people I love hurt by my mistakes, or I need to make a different choice. The girl I was dating during all of that, well, her life was turned upside down. She was in her first year of college, and she was basically alone and had to go through a pregnancy, a birth, and then she had to let go of that baby. She will never, ever be the same. Also, think about that baby. That baby is a human being and deserved two loving parents. We believe that she got that, but the heartache of knowing she was given up for adoption will affect her one day. Our parents were also gravely affected. They had to grieve the loss of a grandchild they would never know.

"I had believed," Shane continued, "that my choices were just that—mine. I felt that people should stay out of my life and let me make my decisions and my mistakes if I wanted to. But I couldn't have been more wrong. My personal and most private decisions affected everyone

I cared about. The hardest part of facing my consequences was watching the people I loved suffer. And there was nothing I could do about it. . .it was too late."

Finishing up his testimony, Shane turned it over to Jodie, one of the cheerleaders. She shared a much different experience. "I was in high school, a junior at the time, and I wanted to date a boy who was a junior in college. My parents forbade me to see him because he was too old and there was something about him they just didn't like, but they couldn't quite identify what it was. I thought that they were just being judgmental and were wrong, so I sneaked around and dated him anyway. To make a very long story short, one night he slipped something into my cola; and when I became affected by the drug, he raped me.

"My parents had been right; but they couldn't convince me, so I ignored them. In retrospect I wonder just who I thought I was. I mean, what arrogance I must have had to think that I knew more than them. If only I had just heeded their warning and obeyed their wishes, I would have avoided a lifetime of pain. I suffered tremendous loss, years of anguish, and it took years of counseling before I felt somewhat whole again. It wasn't until I found the Lord that I really began to love myself again and feel restored to a level of innocence that had been stripped from me.

"The main thing that I'd like for you to take from my story is that you are all just like me. You think you know so much and that your parents are old-fashioned, right? Don't buy into that lie from the enemy. He wants you to believe that you know better, because when you question your parents and doubt their word and are willing to disobey them, that's when he can sneak in and get control of your life. Who do you want to be in control of your life? Choose God, and then let Him work through your parents to lead you down the right road."

They continued on with the testimonies, and when they had about thirty minutes left in the evening, Shane stood up again and said, "We're going to try something a little different. We'd like to separate into two groups. The boys will come with me and the other players outside, and the girls will stay here with Jodie and Becky. We thought that it might give you all a little more freedom to talk about the things that really matter most to you and also to give us the opportunity to address issues that pertain to girls and boys separately. How does that sound?"

With a chorus of agreement, the students began to shuffle positions—the boys went outside and the girls arranged their seating so that they were a little more comfortable and their circle a little tighter.

Jodie started off the question-and-answer time by saying, "Do any of you have a topic or a question that you'd like to ask us?"

Dani raised her hand. "I have a question. It's really a two-parter, if that's okay." When they nodded and said it was fine, she continued. "Were you both on the cheerleading squad and really popular in high school? And if so, do you think the popularity influenced you in making poor decisions?"

"Great question. Do you want to answer that, Becky?"

"Yeah, for me it was definitely a factor. I loved my position on the squad, and it did help me become very popular in school. In that role, I made some bad choices so that I would look cool and keep my 'popular status.' I was a leader in both the good things and in the bad things."

"Same for me," Jodie said. "I wanted to be

popular, and cheerleading helped me get there; but it took a lot of dumb decisions and mistakes to keep me there. I just wish I had known that the people who wanted me to behave that way weren't really my friends. If I had really understood that, it may have made it easier to say no to some things."

"How about some other questions?"

"I have one." A new girl named Megan raised her hand. "My boyfriend has been pressuring me to go further with him physically than I feel comfortable going. What do you think I should do?"

"Honestly," Jodie said, "I think you should find a new boyfriend. If you are with someone who is pressuring you to do anything at all, then he doesn't really, truly care about you. He's only interested in how you can benefit him. If he really cared about you, he would care about what you're ready for or not ready for. Plus, if you have a spiritual foundation and you're trying to follow God's will, wouldn't you want someone who supported that and wanted the same thing?"

"But," Megan asked, "aren't all boys like that? I mean, are there any who wouldn't put the pressure on?"

"Of course there are. There are boys here in this meeting tonight who are worried about protecting their own purity. Those are the kinds of boys you want to be with."

"So, maybe where I meet them is part of the problem?" Megan was looking for clarification, and all of the other girls were hanging on Jodie's words.

"Well, you can meet a good boy at school and a bad seed at church. The location isn't a guarantee, but it sure is a good start. But girls, let's consider something else entirely. What if you didn't have a boyfriend at all right now? You know, God has a perfect plan for your life. He set aside this period of growing up to be the time when He shapes you into the confident, secure, and godly woman that He wants you to be. That process is so much more difficult if you're already trying to act like an adult and have adult relationships. I mean, do you really think that you will meet and date a boy now who will become your husband later? If you don't think so, then what's the point of dating now? You're only opening yourself up for hardship and pain." Jodie paused and looked around the group, making eye contact with as many girls as possible.

"If I sound opinionated on this subject, it's because I am. I only wish someone could have gotten through to me when I was your age. I wish I had spent less time acting like a grown-up and more time actually growing up. I let my identity be shaped by whether or not boys liked me. I forgot that I am perfect and beautiful in God's eyes already. Don't make the same mistake I did, okay?"

They continued talking until it was time to go home. When it was over, Drew and Dani picked up their purses and started to head for the door. "Hang on a second, Dani. I want to talk to Jodie privately." Drew ran over to Jodie and told her that she was fantastic.

Jodie said, "You have that look in your eye, Drew. The same look I had when I was your age. I just hope you remember some of the things we said tonight. Here, take my e-mail address. If you ever find that you're in need of someone to talk to, shoot me a note. Okay?"

"Thanks so much. I really appreciate you guys coming here and doing this. It was awesome." They briefly hugged, and then Drew was on her way to find her family. She was much more excited about having had the chance to meet real cheerleaders than she was about anything they had said. She put Jodie's e-mail address in her wallet in a safe place, just in case she needed it sometime.

Chapter 5

IS IT A DATE?

The bleachers were full, and the crowd roared. It was the first home game of the season. Students, family members, and locals had all turned out wearing their Panthers shirts and hats, and waved their flags in support of the football team. The vendors made their way through the throng of people selling their hot dogs and popcorn. Young kids played under and behind the bleachers. Dani and her parents got there early enough to find seats in the fourth row and were all eager to support Drew at her first game.

Dani couldn't help herself; she got into the excitement of the event and the energy that the crowd was creating. She sat forward in her seat and tried to find Drew among the cheerleaders on the sidelines. They huddled in a circle, getting a pep talk from the captain. . .oh, wait. It was Drew giving the pep talk; she *was* the captain. All of a sudden, feelings of jealousy and resentment started to fade away as Dani became proud of her sister. She watched her sister lead the squad; Drew was right where she was supposed to be. Dani vowed to herself that, from then on, she would support Drew and encourage her.

The cheerleaders all let out a little yell for team spirit and then broke to begin their opening cheer. The junior varsity squad customarily opened with a cheer-and-dance routine to set the tone for the game. Then they spent their time during the game on the sidelines cheering for their team and leading the crowd. So, at five minutes before kick-off, they took off their sweatshirts and bounded out onto the field into their formation.

"Ready! Begin!" Drew shouted off the cue to start the routine. Music started and the girls began their dance. They were perfectly in sync and looked fantastic on the field in their red and gold skirts that floated around their thighs, and their sleeveless white shirts with the yellow and black chevron that said PANTHERS in the middle. Even

Dani had to admit that they really looked cool. In the middle of the routine, there was a pause in the music and the girls began a cheer for their team. It was exciting and stirred up the crowd's energy even more. The music began just as the cheer ended, and they finished up their dance routine with a pyramid. In front of the pyramid, Drew ran and did a round-off and two back flips to finish up the routine with a flourish.

The crowd was worked into a frenzy. The JV cheerleaders had been exciting to watch, a more talented group than any JV team before them. It set the tone for the whole event. "I can't believe how great those girls were," Mom leaned over and said to her husband and Dani.

"I know, Mom. Drew really looks like she was meant to be doing that, doesn't she?"

"I've never been so proud of her," Dad said. "Looks like all of those years of dance and gymnastics have paid off. And it's not just that, she's a real leader. Those girls look up to her."

"I'm really happy for Drew, and I feel bad for being so upset about it all. But I do hope that I can find my niche somehow," Dani admitted.

"You will, sweetie," Mom promised. "You'll figure out what excites you and gives you the same joy that Drew has found. It might be a sport, a club, or maybe something academic like debate team or the class play."

"Oh, I like the sound of debate team, Mom. I might have to look into that."

"Dani, that's a great idea," Dad encouraged. "If you're serious about becoming a lawyer one day, debate team would be a great experience for you."

Dani sat back, deep in thought as she contemplated the possibilities and recognized that being different from her sister might not be as horrible as she had once thought.

While they were on the bleachers, waiting for the cheerleaders to come out at halftime, Drew was on the sidelines cheering for the team. Every once in a while, she took a break to get a drink of water from the team cooler. Whenever she went for a drink, her family couldn't see her inside the team shelter. So they also couldn't see the boy she was talking to every chance she got.

Whenever she saw that he wasn't playing on the field, she went to get a drink of water; and each time, he was standing right there by the cooler—Trevor Jaymes. The sight of him made Drew get a little jittery, but she knew she had to play it cool. She confidently walked right up to the cooler and drew some water out into a cup that was provided.

"Hi, boys." Without looking directly at Trevor, she tossed her hair over her shoulders and left the shelter to join her team. Out of the corner of her eye, she could tell that they were watching her; and it seemed that they were talking about her, too. She was very careful not to let them know that she was paying attention to them.

A little while later, before the halftime show, Drew went back for another drink of water. She timed it perfectly so that she would already be there when Trevor got pulled from the game for a rest. He'd had a perfect game so far; but he would wear out if he didn't get a break, and the team needed him fresh to finish up the game later. He came into the team shelter to get a drink of water just as Drew finished filling up her cup.

"Well, hello again, Drew."

"Hi, Trevor. Great game," Drew said enthusiastically. It was time to let her guard down a little so that, if he were interested in her, he would know there was a chance at gaining her attention.

"Thanks a lot," he replied with surprise. "I didn't think you cheerleaders even watched the game."

"Ha, funny. Of course we do. How else would we know when to cheer?"

"Well, you might, but I guarantee you that half of your team just waits for your cue and follows suit. But at least you're watching me. . . er. . .I mean us."

"Oh, I'm watching, all right," Drew replied flirtatiously as she walked back to her squad.

"Hey, Steph, what's the score?" she asked her teammate as a test to see if she was watching.

"Um, well, a minute ago it was, um. . .I'm not sure."

Hmm, Drew thought, surprised that Stephanie hadn't been paying attention, since the coach had just stressed the importance of that at their last practice. *I'm going to have to keep an eye on that and maybe even bring it up again in practice.* They were there to support the team, and it was much more credible if they actually knew why they were cheering.

The game continued on, and Drew had a blast. Her family did, too, and they watched her throughout the entire game. She was definitely in her element. The halftime show was perfect. It was mainly the varsity cheerleaders, but the JV squad also had several parts in the routine which turned it into a great big field show.

Drew was exhausted when the game was over and was about ready to head to the car to meet her family after she had packed up her things. She suddenly felt a presence behind her and turned to see Trevor watching her, waiting to be noticed.

"Hey. What's up?" Drew asked casually.

"Well, Miss Daniels, I was wondering if you'd like to grab a bite to eat. A bunch of us are going to The Grill. I can have you home in about an hour, give or take a few considering the crowds."

"I'd love to. Let me go tell my parents and sister that I'll be home soon." Drew didn't tell him that she would have to beg and perhaps even tell a little white lie to get permission. But there was no way she wasn't going to go. She ran quickly over to her family who were waiting for her at the car.

"Sweetie, you were awesome." Mom pulled her into a tight hug.

"I agree, Drew," Dad chimed in. "You were

definitely in your element. I've never been more proud of you."

"Me, too, sis. I'm sorry I've given you a hard time about it all. You're clearly doing what you are supposed to be doing," Dani admitted.

Drew was thrilled to hear their comments but didn't want to keep Trevor waiting. She hated that she'd have to lie. . .but it wasn't really a total lie. . .she hoped.

"Thanks, everyone. Mom, Dad, I'd like to go with the team and get a bite to eat. It's kind of customary, and being the captain, I should probably be there. We're going to The Grill, and I'd be home in about an hour depending on how busy it is. Is that okay?"

"Sure, sweetie. An adult will give you a ride home? If not, be sure to call for a ride. Okay?" When Drew promised that she would, her mom asked, "Hey, can Dani go?"

"No way, Mom," Dani jumped in, much to Drew's relief. "This isn't my thing. I'm not tagging along. I don't even want to go anyway. I'm too tired."

Drew hugged everyone and then went back to find the group. To her surprise, everyone was gone except for Trevor. "You ready? They're saving seats for us."

"Yep, all set. Let me grab my bags, and we can go."

The Grill was bustling with excitement as the football team and cheerleaders filled the rich mahogany booths. They were all starving after the big game and were excited over their win. Spirits were high, and the noise level was deafening. Drew and Trevor navigated through the high fives and congratulatory claps on the back as Trevor's teammates congratulated him on the win. His big, toothy grin revealed just how much he reveled in the recognition.

The crowd pressed in so tightly that it was difficult for the two to squeeze through, and Trevor kept losing Drew as people swarmed around him. Finally, he just grabbed her hand and held on until they finally made their way to their seats. "Phew," Trevor said as they slid into the booth. "We made it."

"Yep, it was looking kind of iffy there for a minute." Drew laughed.

"Hey, Drew, I haven't had a chance to tell you this yet." Trevor leaned over the table and said privately, "You did a really great job tonight."

"Oh yeah," Buck said, overhearing Trevor's words.

"You really did do a great job. I've never seen the JV squad look so awesome," Buck's girlfriend, Sam, added.

"Trevor said you were cute the day he bumped into you accidentally, *wink, wink,* but I had no idea that he was talking about the captain of the cheerleaders." Buck revealed a little more about Trevor's little accident than Trevor would have liked, judging by his reddened face.

"I didn't know she was even going out for cheerleading that day. I thought she was just a cute freshman."

"That's enough about me." Drew laughed, her face reddening. "This is getting awkward. I'm right here."

"Okay, fair enough. We'll talk about you later then," Buck teased.

"Don't let him get to you. He only picks on people he likes," Sam informed Drew.

"Oh, I think I can hold my own." Drew laughed again. "But I'm starving. I wonder if we even have time to order, though. I have to be home in about an hour."

"Food's on its way. We already ordered." Buck was proud to surprise them.

"Good move, dude. This crowd is crazy."

At that moment, the waitress appeared at their table and set down Cokes for Trevor and Drew and cheeseburgers and fries all around. They dug in with a vengeance, and all conversation stopped. A cheeseburger had never tasted so good.

After they had eaten, it was time for Trevor to get Drew home. On the way to the car he said, "We'd better get you home so that your parents trust me for the next time we go out."

"Oh?" Drew coyly asked. "What makes you so sure there's going to be a next time?"

"Well, I mean, only if you want to. . ." Trevor stammered.

"Oh, well, in *that* case," Drew teased, "I'm sure there will be many next times."

Trevor visibly relaxed when he heard that and, without thinking, reached over and took her hand. Drew had never had her hand held by a boy she liked—and she enjoyed the little tingle of excitement it gave her. She giggled just as they reached the car. Trevor tucked her into her seat and shut her door, then went around to the other side. Before he got in, Drew wiped the dampness off her hand and placed it on the console between the two seats—just in case he'd like to hold it again.

He held her hand in silence—they were both taking in the moment and were lost in thought, so they forgot to speak out loud—the whole way to her house. As they pulled into her driveway, Drew turned to Trevor and thanked him for a great time. He promised to call her but would also see her in school Monday.

Drew hurriedly got out of the car so that her parents wouldn't come to the door and see that she was alone in the car with a boy. She ran into the house excitedly and started talking the moment she got into the living room where her parents were. She began filling them in with all sorts of needless details about who was there, what they ate, how busy it was, how fun it was to be a part of the team. . .so they wouldn't think to question her about who drove her home. They were tired, so it worked. Drew excused herself to head upstairs to bed, and Dani, who had been sitting on the couch, followed her up.

"I saw you pull in the driveway. You're going to need to be more careful, sis," Dani warned. "You're making some important choices, and you've never been one to lie to Mom and Dad or disobey so blatantly."

"I didn't lie. . .they didn't even ask how I got home."

"Not telling the truth is the same as lying. And you did break one of their rules—several, actually. You led them to believe that you could be trusted. Just think hard next time about whether or not it's really worth it to lose that trust or even damage it a little. I just don't want to see you get hurt."

Dani heard her softly snoring. "Drew. . . Drew. . .you there?"

But Drew had fallen asleep already. Chuckling to herself, Dani rolled over and said a little prayer for her sister before nodding off herself.

Chapter 6

GOD'S WAY

The girls awoke to the smell of bacon, as they normally did every Sunday morning before church. Drew and Dani were both very tired after a long weekend that started with game night on Friday and continued with family activities on Saturday. They pulled their matching comforters up over their heads and attempted to bury themselves under the covers to get a few more minutes of sleep. Their mom knocked softly on the door before she opened it. Coming into the room, she opened the window shades to let in some light, and the girls groaned when the brightness hit their eyes.

"Mom, we need just a few more minutes, ple–e–e–ease?" Drew begged.

"Now girls, it's time to get ready for church. Don't make me lower your curfew—I'll do that if church becomes affected by your staying up too late on the weekends."

"All right, all right, I'm getting up." Drew put forth an effort by sitting up in her bed. Dani already had her feet on the floor and was sitting on the side of her bed. "We'll be down in a few minutes, Mom."

"Now girls, don't lie back down," Mom warned them as she left the room. It took all of Drew's effort, amid a lot of sleepy moaning and eye rubbing, to continue getting up when all she wanted to do was to crawl back under the covers.

Slowly, both girls got out of their beds and headed for the bathroom they shared. Silently, Dani brushed her teeth and washed her face while Drew got her things together for a shower.

"We really need to wake up," Drew said.

"Yeah, we sure do. I can't believe how tired I am," Dani admitted.

"Yesterday was a big day. But we better get it together, or Mom and Dad aren't going to be happy. We have to show them that we can handle being up late and not struggle in the morning. It will help our cause for staying out later and going on dates."

"Um, *our* cause?" Dani laughed. "That's *your* cause right now, sis. Not me. I have nothing to do with it."

"Oh, believe me, your day will come. . .and you'll be so glad that I paved the way by getting them on our side now."

"Whatever you say." Dani laughed again, shaking her head. "Mom and Dad aren't going to just let you start dating and staying out late, you know. When are you going to tell them about Trevor, anyway?"

"When there's something to tell, I guess." Drew looked annoyed.

"Oh, I'm pretty sure Mom and Dad would feel that line had been crossed already." She put up her hand to keep Drew from defending herself any further. "I just hope you know what you're doing. I care about what happens to you, and I don't want to see you get hurt."

Drew looked at the reflection staring back at her from the mirror—sometimes she forgot whether she was looking at herself or her sister. To whichever one it was, or maybe to both of them, she confidently said, "I have everything under control."

Drew jumped in to take a quick shower to help wake her up. Dani continued getting ready in silence. The silence started to get to Drew, so she decided that it was up to her to break the ice and get her sister cheered up. She unhooked the shower massage head and turned the water from hot to very cold. She quietly reached forward and pulled back the curtain.

Being careful not to get Dani's hair wet, because that would just be cruel, she aimed the wet, pulsating stream at Dani's body, soaking her pajamas with icy cold water. Dani shrieked in surprise when the water hit her skin. At first she looked angry, but when she saw Drew's face all aglow with mischief, she dissolved into laughter. It was a tension breaker they both needed.

"You just wait! I'll get you back when you least expect it," Dani warned.

"I look forward to it, sis." Drew's eyes twinkled as she returned to her shower, and Dani had a big smile on her face as she toweled off before leaving the bathroom to get dressed.

" 'I have everything under control,' " the preacher began his sermon. "Do we say that to God? If we don't come right out and say it, don't we act like it sometimes? You know, we have access to God's plan all laid out for us. We have His perfect guidelines, and we *know* His will. We know which actions grieve Him, and there is seldom a question about what is right in His eyes. We get all of that information, that insight into who He is and what He wants for us and from us, right from His Word, the Bible. Yet, we often walk through life acting as though we have no clue about what to do. We say with our words and our actions that we have everything under control—basically, that we are going to ignore God's desires and plans for us because we know better. What drives that mindset? I'll tell you what it is—it's pure selfishness. It's a heart that is closed off to the will of God and is selfishly pursuing personal plans and desires while forsaking God in the process.

"Do you find yourself in a situation where you know that what you are doing is wrong, yet you turn off the inner voice that cries out to your spirit? Do you ignore God because you are so dead set on doing whatever it is that you want to do?"

Dani and Drew sat next to each other; they looked like almost the same person. However, they had completely different postures as they listened to the preacher. Dani sat with her head down, thinking. She was hoping that her sister was listening; and she was deeply worried that Drew wouldn't hear the preacher's message, a message that she obviously needed to hear. Dani worried that Drew was so eager to experience this new life that she wanted so badly that she'd ignore the Holy Spirit and get herself into trouble.

Drew, on the other hand, was sitting quietly, looking at her fingernails, digging in her purse for a piece of gum, staying busy rather than truly listening to the words of the pastor. She had heard enough and, even though she knew that he was technically correct, it wasn't a message that she wanted to hear or was willing to do anything about at that moment.

"Sit up and listen, Drew." Mrs. Daniels nudged her, trying to get her to take interest in the sermon. "Stop fidgeting so much," she whispered to her daughter.

Drew was very happy when the sermon was over and the congregation rose to their feet to sing a closing chorus. On the way out, they shook the hands of the people they passed; and as they approached the pastor, they paused to say hello. Mr. Daniels shook his hand and said, "Great sermon today, Pastor. You really hit home with this one."

"I'm very glad you got something out of it. How about you, young lady?" Pastor Michaels asked Drew.

She wondered if he had noticed her inattention. "I thought you did a good job, too." Drew didn't quite know what to say.

"Oh, I'm not looking for compliments on my speaking ability. I was wondering if the message reached you in any way."

"Sure, it did. It's important to do what God wants us to do and not only what we want to do," Drew answered, glad that she had heard at least part of the sermon but frustrated to be put on the spot like that.

"It sounds like you did hear something after all. Just be sure that you take it seriously, young lady. They are nice words, but the truth behind them is what's powerful."

"Yes, sir. Thank you." Drew couldn't wait to escape the scrutiny.

"Man, I feel like I just got into trouble," Drew complained as they walked to the car.

"Drew, it was clear that you weren't paying any attention. I was even a bit embarrassed. Perhaps the pastor sensed that it was a message you needed to hear," Drew's mom suggested.

"I don't know why. I was just bored."

"You still need to respect Pastor Michaels enough that you pay attention and don't become a distraction."

Realizing that she wasn't helping herself at all with her current attitude, Drew relented. "You're right, Mom. Sorry about that."

"It's okay, sweetie. Just make sure you don't do that again. Now where should we go eat?" Mom asked, changing the subject.

"I vote for Shakey's," Dani jumped in, suggesting the pizza buffet.

"Sounds good to me," Drew agreed.

"I'll go for that, too," Dad said.

"Sounds like it's unanimous. Shakey's it is."

They arrived at their favorite restaurant, and, as starved as they were, they were thrilled that it was a buffet so they didn't have to wait for their food to be cooked and brought to their table. As they were being seated, they passed two students from school who were there with their families. They both said hello to Drew but ignored Dani.

Pretending not to notice or care, Dani slid into the booth first, followed by Drew and their parents on the other side. They made several trips to the buffet and enjoyed a leisurely lunch.

"I have news," Dani said.

"News? We've been together all weekend. How could you have something new to tell us that we haven't heard already?" Drew laughed.

"Well, I guess it's more of an announcement than news, so far anyway."

"The suspense is killing me. What is it?" Drew prodded.

"I have decided to try out for the debate team," Dani announced, then sat back in her seat to wait for the comments. She was visibly happy with herself for coming to that decision.

"That's great, sweetheart. When did you decide?" Mom asked.

"Ever since we talked about it the other day, I haven't been able to stop thinking about it. I just think it's something I would be good at and I would enjoy. Plus, like Dad said, it will only help my college transcripts."

"I'm all for it," Dad encouraged. "And I do think you'll be terrific at it."

"That's awesome, sis. I think it definitely

is your thing. When are tryouts? Can we be there?"

"Aw, thanks for even wanting to be...," Dani began but was interrupted by Drew.

"Of course we want to support you. I can't wait to come watch you argue with people. It'll be awesome." Drew laughed.

"They're Tuesday after school. I almost missed them, so it's a really good thing that we discussed it when we did. I had to dig up the calendar of events that we got when school started. Now I just have to practice as much as possible before then. Do you guys want to help me practice, maybe?"

"Definitely. How do you practice for that, though?" Drew wondered.

"I looked online at the types of categories and contests that are part of a typical debate-team event. The one that sounds the most interesting to me are debates where you have to blindly select a controversial category, like legalizing drugs, for example, and begin to argue one side of the debate. Then, when the bell rings, you have to flip and argue the other side—all with no preparation. Then you're scored for how per- suasive you were on both sides of the argument. Talk about thinking on your feet." Dani laughed. "So maybe you guys could pick some topics and then help me figure out how to formulate arguments for the multiple sides of the debate. What do you think?"

Everyone agreed that it sounded like fun and even kind of fascinating. They all agreed to help that evening and Monday night, as well.

"This is going to be a fun year for us," Mom said to her husband. "These girls are going to keep us busy with their activities, but at least they are both so very interesting."

"Oh, I completely agree. It's going to be a great year. We should learn a lot from these two."

Chapter 7

FAMOUS LAST WORDS

"Drew, phone for you," Dad called up the stairs. "Who's calling, please?"

"My name is Trevor, sir. I go to school with Drew."

"Hello, Trevor. Have we met?"

"No, sir, but I look forward to meeting you," Trevor said politely just as they heard a *click* on the other end of the phone line.

"Dad, I'm on the phone now. You can hang up," Drew impatiently said from the up-stairs phone. Once her dad had hung up the receiver, Drew excitedly said, "Trevor, it's great to hear from you. What's going on?"

"Oh, nothing much. I was just thinking about how much fun we had the other night, and

I thought I'd give you a call to see if you were thinking the same thing." Trevor sounded shy.

"Yeah, to be honest, I haven't thought about much else since."

"Me, too." Drew wasn't used to being so open and vulnerable and, though it felt good and very grown-up, it was a little awkward.

"So what have you been doing today, Drew?"

"I went to church with my family and then out to eat lunch. Just now Dani and I were in our room working on homework. How about you?"

"I slept in until about eleven, and I've been playing video games since I got up. Just kind of a lazy day."

"Sometimes those are the best kind of days, especially after a night like Friday."

"I agree, and at least I didn't have to get up to go to church. Do you have to go every Sunday?"

"Yeah, believe it or not, we go every Sunday morning and every Wednesday night, too. But Wednesday night is for youth group, which is fun. You should come sometime."

"Man, I don't know if I could take that much church. I'm lucky that my parents don't make us go. Do you hate it?"

"No, I wouldn't say I hate it. I sure would

have preferred to sleep in this morning, though." Drew laughed and then felt a little guilty for not standing up for her family's values and supporting her church rather than almost mocking it with her comments. She wasn't sure what to say next to repair her previous statements. She decided a change in subjects was a good idea. "So, do you have any brothers or sisters, Trevor?"

"I have two little brothers and one little sister. My sister is almost two years old, and the boys are in between."

"That's a lot of kids." Drew laughed. "Do you like having little kids around or is it a pain?"

"It's not so bad. . .sometimes. It definitely has its moments. You'll have to meet them someday soon."

"I'd love to meet them."

Drew wasn't very practiced in these types of conversations, so another slightly awkward silence followed. She twisted the phone cord between her fingers until Trevor spoke up again.

"So, you have a twin sister, huh?" When Drew said yes, he went on. "Is that weird? I mean, what's it like to have someone who looks just like you?"

"It's pretty cool. I mean, my sister will always

be my best friend. But even though we look alike, we have different personalities and interests. We're just now starting to figure that out and do some things separately. Before, we did everything exactly the same."

"Do people ever get you mixed up?"

"Yeah, that used to happen a lot. It doesn't happen as much since I changed my hair, and I think that we just act differently lately."

"Did you ever try to mix people up?"

"Oh, yeah. We've had lots of fun with that. We used to go to each other's classes and try to mix up the teachers. It almost always worked. Once in a while we'd slip up and get caught. It was always funny, though." Drew laughed at the memory. "One time, at summer Bible camp, we spent the whole week messing people up just for fun. We would switch beds and change our clothes midday. It was definitely a diversion in what had been kind of a boring week other than that."

"Well, at the risk of you two doing that to me, I'll take my chances and ask if you want to go on a real date with me on Saturday night," Trevor asked with a nervous tremor.

Drew laughed out loud. "Oh don't worry, I wouldn't trick you like that, and I don't think it would work anymore, anyway. But of course, I'd love to go out with you on Saturday," Drew answered, not telling him that she wouldn't be allowed to go on a date. She was determined to find a way to get permission. "I'll let you know in school tomorrow, just so I can make sure that my family doesn't have any other plans. Otherwise, it would be perfect."

"Great. I have to run for now, though," Trevor said. "So, I'll see you in school tomorrow?"

"You bet. Thanks for calling."

Drew hung up the phone and sat quietly for a moment, contemplating the conversation she just had. The cutest and most popular boy in school had just called her and asked her out on a date. But her parents would never let her go, she realized with a sinking feeling.

Drew considered all of her options. Maybe they would let her go if it were a group of kids— no, she quickly dismissed that idea. Even the idea of a group date would be quickly rejected by her parents. Maybe if she were honest with Trevor and invited him over to her house, they would get to have their "date" and her parents would get a chance to get to know him—no, that wouldn't work, either. Then she would have to admit to Trevor that she wasn't allowed to date. Drew wondered how she could ever avoid him knowing that. She needed some more time to ease into this and get her parents on her side, so she hoped that they had plans for Saturday night. Friday night would be game night and Sunday night was a school night; so if she could just get out of her "date" with Trevor for Saturday night, then she'd have a whole week before next weekend to work something out—which she fully intended to do.

"Dani, we need to talk. I need your help," Drew announced as she walked back into their bedroom and flopped on her own bed across the room from her sister.

Dani looked up from the book that she was reading and raised her eyebrows in question. "What's up?"

"Trevor asked me to go out on a date with him on Saturday night."

"I don't know how I can help with *that*." Dani frowned as she put her book down. "You know it's not going to happen. Besides, we have plans for Saturday night. It's Grandma's birthday, remember?"

"It is?" Drew practically shouted in relief. "That's great!"

"How is that great? I thought you were happy he asked you out."

"Oh, I'm happy, that's for sure. But I think I need more time to figure out how to get permission."

"Drew. . ." Dani leaned forward and lowered her voice in seriousness. "What's the big deal? Why do you want to rush it so much? Why not just leave it alone?"

"You just don't understand. Trevor is the cutest boy in school, probably the most popular, too. Going out with him would really help me make a name for myself."

"You don't need *him* to make a name for yourself. . .whatever that means. You're awesome all by yourself."

"I want more, Dani. You just don't understand."

"I get that you think you want something 'more,' but I just don't understand what that means. More of what?"

"I want to be popular. I want to have tons of friends. I want recognition and for people to know my name. I want to be prom queen one day. This is all part of making those plans a reality."

"So, poor Trevor is just a way for you to get the popularity you want? Is that fair to him?"

"It's not like that. I really do like him. Have you seen how cute he is? He is totally fun and has a great sense of humor, too. Plus, I like the way it feels when he holds my hand."

"What? He held your hand?" Dani was shocked her sister would have let things go so far with a boy she hardly knew. "Oh, Drew, this is going so fast. You really need to think about what you're doing."

"I have everything under control. Don't worry about me." Drew patted Dani on her leg as she got up to leave the room. Dani just wasn't ready for the changes that Drew was experiencing.

"Famous last words, Drew. Famous last words."

Chapter 8

PEP RALLY

"Oh, how cute you look." Mom grinned when she saw Drew dressed for school on Monday morning. It was Pep-Rally Monday—a tradition for the third week of school. It was a way to recognize the football team and cheerleaders and build school spirit and team support. As part of the event, it was an unspoken understanding that the players and cheerleaders would wear their home-game uniforms to school for the day.

Drew was so excited about it, which was obvious by her big grin as she bounced into the kitchen. She was wearing her short-sleeved, tight, white cheerleading top that said PANTHERS down the right side with a gold and red chevron on the chest. The little cheerleading skirt was the shortest skirt Drew had ever worn. Brick red with gold cording around the hem, it flounced around her upper thighs as she swayed through the room. Her clean, white sneakers and white ankle socks finished off the outfit. Her hair was tied back in a ponytail and secured with a gold ribbon, and she was wearing the extra make-up that her parents agreed she could wear for cheering events, unaware that she wore it every day, anyway. Drew was the perfect picture of a wholesome athlete, and her smile proved her happiness.

"This is going to be such a fun day. You're still going to come, right, Mom?"

"Of course, honey. I wouldn't miss it for the world. I'll be at the school by one thirty to get a good seat. Now, you'd better eat something and get ready to go before you're late. Where's your sister?"

"Dani says she doesn't feel good. She's dressed, but she says she isn't going to school."

"What? Really? I'd better go check on her." Mom left in a hurry to check on her daughter. She was sure that illness wasn't really Dani's problem.

A few minutes later, Dani and her mom were

walking into the kitchen, smiling. Whatever had been ailing Dani must have passed, because she looked just fine to Drew. "You ready, sis? Big day today. We need to go." Drew was so excited she could hardly contain her energy.

Drew spent a few minutes talking with Trevor in the hallway before first period. But just as quickly as they had started chatting, the bell rang, signaling that they had two minutes to be in their seats for their first class. "Oops, better run. I'll catch you at the pep rally later."

"You bet," Drew said. "See you then." They turned and ran off in separate directions to their classes. They didn't share any classes because they were two years apart. They did luck out and get the same lunch hour, though. But Drew wouldn't see Trevor for lunch that day because the football team was having a pre-rally meeting. So she was on her own until later. Racing through the hall to get to her class, Drew could tell that the other girls were looking at her with envy, and the boys were looking her up and down, checking out how she looked in her cheerleading uniform. This had to be the best day ever.

"Hey, Drew. How's it going?" Sam, one of

the varsity cheerleaders she met at The Grill last Friday night, slid into the seat next to her just before the bell rang. They had their homeroom class first, which was the perfect time to finish up homework from the day before, study for any tests or quizzes that would be given that day, or to quietly chitchat with a neighbor. But that day, Drew was too riled up to settle down to school-work, so she welcomed Sam's company.

"I'm great. You ready for the pep rally?" Drew asked

"Oh yeah, it's going to be so cool. You look great today, by the way." When Drew thanked her, she continued. "So, I hear you and Trevor have become a hot item."

"News travels fast, doesn't it?"

"So it's true? You're together now?" Sam seemed impressed.

"I suppose so. He's asked me out on a date, and he wants to hang out all of the time. I don't know that I would say that anything is official, though."

"What a major development for freshman year. Way to go."

Drew, proud of herself but wanting to stay cool, answered, "Well, we'll see. He still has to pass a few tests."

"Are you kidding me? He's perfect. What tests could you possibly be talking about?"

"Oh, I don't know. I haven't thought of them yet." Drew laughed at her admission. "I'm pretty much kidding. He is kind of perfect, isn't he?" The girls dissolved into fits of giggles until their teacher reminded them to keep it down.

The cheerleading coach was grinning from ear to ear as she got her squads ready for the pep rally. "Girls, this is going to be a phenomenal year. It's one of those times when everything has just fallen into place and it makes magic. Our football teams are so talented and stand a great chance of making it to the championships, the cheerleading squads are the most talented and creative teams I've ever had the privilege of coaching, and the school and community are energized and behind us like never before. That gymnasium is packed with people from throughout the community who have come here today to soak in *your* spirit. You girls, more than anyone else, drive the energy and the spirit that supports our teams and our schools. You need to go out there today with nothing on your mind other than getting energy from that crowd. Are you ready, girls?"

Every girl let out a shout of excitement, each one ready to not only raise school spirit but also to soak it in from the crowd. Drew's heart was beating so fast; she was eager but nervous.

Finally, the double doors to the gym opened, and the cheerleaders were introduced first. The JV team was brought out before the varsity team. Each girl was introduced by name, at which time she would come into the gym, running the length of the gym floor, shaking her pom-poms and waving to the crowds in the bleachers that lined both sides of the gym. One by one, each girl had her moment to shine in front of the crowd. Drew was introduced last for her team. "And last, but certainly not least, we want you to meet our junior varsity squad captain, Drew Daniels!"

When she heard her name, Drew took off running toward the middle of the gym floor, did a round-off, a back flip, and then turned and waved her pom-poms at the crowd with a big grin on her face. She was a natural, and the crowd loved her energy and her big, beautiful smile. She soaked it all in and then jogged over to the side where her team was lined up.

The varsity team was introduced in the

same way, and those cheerleaders lined up on the other side of the gymnasium. The two teams formed two parallel lines and waited for the big moment—the entrance of the football team. Each player was introduced, and they ran through the lines of cheerleaders to the sounds of cheering, shouting, jumping, and bouncing. The players really seemed buoyed by the experience, and the crowd loved every second of it.

When the introductions were over, the band played the school song and the cheerleaders got into formation and did their signature dance and cheer. The crowd went wild.

In the stands, Dani was sitting with her mom and dad. They were thoroughly enjoying themselves and cheering right along with the rest of the crowd.

"I really had no idea it would be like this," Mrs. Daniels said. "Drew is going to have so many great high school memories if she sticks with this." Mrs. Daniels snapped picture after picture of the celebration.

"Oh, believe me, she'll be sticking with it." Dani wondered if her mom would be so excited for Drew if she knew how serious Drew was getting about a boy—the captain of the football team, no less. Somehow, she doubted it.

Drew and her team moved to the sidelines and cheered as the coaches were introduced. Trevor came to stand by her while the coaches gave rousing speeches meant to continue stirring the crowd. Trevor and Drew stood together and looked comfortable together, like they had known each other for a long time. Dani wondered if her parents were noticing, but she was afraid to look for fear of drawing attention to the couple.

But when Trevor leaned down to whisper something in Drew's ear, Dani couldn't stand it any longer. She tried to look out of the corner of her eye at her mom. Dani's mom slowly lowered the camera to her lap, and she leaned forward a bit. Her mouth was slightly open, and her eyes were wide in surprise. She nudged her husband, nodded toward the scene she was witnessing, and raised her eyebrows in question, wondering if he saw the same thing she did.

"Dani, who is that boy your sister is talking to?" Mom asked.

"That's Trevor Jaymes. He's the captain of the football team."

"Oh, he's the boy who called the other day, isn't he?" Mr. Daniels asked.

"Is he a freshman, too?" Mrs. Daniels hoped so, even though it was clear that he was not.

"No, he's a junior, Mom. He's a nice guy, though."

"I'm sure he is. . . ." Mrs. Daniels didn't ask any further questions at that time, but Dani knew that they would stew in her head and she would have a lot to ask Drew later. Dani hoped she wouldn't be around for that conversation.

Down on the floor, Trevor was asking Drew if she wanted to be his girlfriend. He understood that with their schedules there wouldn't be much time for actual dates; but they would have a lot of time together due to their athletic activities, and they would fit private dates in wherever they could.

Drew beamed with pride and excitement. "Of course I want to be your girlfriend, Trevor. I really like being with you, and I think this year is going to be a blast."

"Great. It's settled then." As a joke, he held up his hand for a high five.

She laughed and slapped his hand with a flourish. She was glad he didn't try to seal the deal with a kiss or something. That was definitely not something she wanted to experience for the first time on a crowded gym floor in front of hundreds of people—including her parents.

It was six o'clock before Drew got home after practice that evening. She was eager to hear what her family had to say about the rally. It had been way too crowded and noisy to try to find them to chat after the rally was over, but she was sure they'd have a lot to say now. She was also a little nervous to find out if her parents had seen anything when she and Trevor were talking on the sidelines. Maybe it would be a good thing, a way to ease them into the idea. She knew, though, that she'd have to be careful how hard she pushed them at first. They would need time to get used to the idea.

"Hi, everyone, I'm home!" Drew announced as she walked into the house after practice. When she arrived at the entryway to the kitchen, she said, "Wow, Mom. It smells so good in here. I'm completely famished."

"I figured you would be. I made your favorite—manicotti and garlic bread."

"Oh, that's awesome. Let's eat!"

Over dinner, they were abuzz about the day's goings-on. "Drew, I have to tell you, I was so proud of you today. I'm so excited for the experience you're going to have in high school." Mom beamed.

"Me, too," Dad said. "I had a good time at the rally, and I think it's wonderful how much school spirit and support is behind your teams. It's inspiring. I'm still not thrilled with those short skirts," he admitted. "But you did look great out there—a real natural."

"Thanks, you guys. I can't believe how much fun I'm having with it all. I really feel like I'm doing what I was meant to be doing right now."

"That much is clear." Mom paused to take a drink of her milk to wash down her food. "There's something else that was clear, too."

Drew groaned inwardly, knowing what was coming. "What's that, Mom?" She feigned innocence.

"It's pretty clear that you and that boy we saw you with have a bit of a crush on each other."

"Who? Trevor?" Drew tried to act shocked, but her mom wasn't buying it.

"You know who I mean. That dreamy boy who was talking to you like there was no one else around. What's the deal there?"

"Well, I guess a crush is a good way to put it. You know how it goes, captain of the football team and cheerleading captain—it's kind of a natural thing."

"It may very well be," her mom said, "but you are quite a bit younger than him. You aren't ready for a relationship like he may be."

Drew shot her sister a look, knowing that Dani must have told Mom how old he was.

Dad, having been quiet until then, jumped in. "I agree, Drew. You are too young to be in a relationship, and you are in the middle of so many other changes right now. Take it one thing at a time."

"It's not like I'm asking to be allowed to go on dates or anything," Drew argued.

"Then what are you asking? Or what are you planning?"

"We just like each other. Neither of us really has time for dates or outside things, so we're just enjoying the fact that we share our team athletics. I am in high school now, and this is part of it. There will probably be other boys as time goes on."

"If that's all it is, I can probably understand that," Mom said. "But don't think it's going to turn into you going on private dates. That won't be happening until you're sixteen, and you know that."

"I know, Mom. What about school-sponsored activities like dances and stuff like that?"

"Oh, that's different. Of course you may go to dances like homecoming and prom. That's all part of getting the full experience of high school; plus, they are chaperoned activities."

Feeling like she had made huge strides, Drew decided that she had better quit while she was ahead. "May I be excused now? I really need to shower, and then I have homework to do." With her parent's agreement, Drew excused herself from the table and headed off for the shower, where she'd have a few moments to herself to daydream about all that had taken place that day. It was a day for the history books.

Chapter 9

INVISIBLE

Dani felt invisible when she was with Drew. Everywhere they went they were met with choruses of, "Hi, Drew." "I like your hair, Drew." "That's a cute shirt, Drew." Everyone seemed to want to talk to Drew and be her friend. They all knew her name, even though Drew knew only a handful of them.

It was much like any celebrity status, Dani realized; people just wanted to make a connection, no matter how small.

Drew squealed next to Dani, making her jump, as Trevor sneaked up behind her and covered her eyes with his hands, saying, "Guess who!"

"I know who it is, silly." Drew giggled, and Dani rolled her eyes.

"You'd better know who it is. I mean, every-one else better keep his hands off," Trevor teased possessively, making Drew smile even wider.

"Hi, Dani. How are you today?" he asked, trying to include Dani.

"Oh, I'm fine, thanks. You?"

"Just fine, now that I've seen my girl."

"I have to run to class. I'll see you two later." Dani scurried off, mainly just to get away from the syrupy sweetness of young love that she was tired of enduring. As an afterthought, she turned to Drew and said, "It's Tuesday, so wait for me out front after school, okay?"

"As always, sis. See ya then," Drew promised, forgetting for a moment why Tuesday was dif-ferent than any other day.

"Finally, a moment alone," Trevor teased, because they were never really alone. Everywhere they went, their friends and other kids wanted their attention. Both of them loved it, though. They seemed made for each other, and everyone saw it.

Though he didn't want to leave Drew, Trevor couldn't afford to be late to class, since the coach always checked up on that. "I'd better get going, too. See you at lunch?"

"Of course. Save me a seat, okay?" Drew had farther to walk to the lunchroom, so Trevor always got there before she did. For a second she considered asking him to save a seat for Dani but then dismissed the idea because she didn't think that Dani would want to sit with Trevor and his friends. It was just not her thing.

Racing to the lunchroom so she'd have as much time as possible, Drew got there in record time. She spotted Trevor and his friends in their usual spot and waved across the room. On her way to meet him, she passed by the table she used to share with her sister, who was already sitting in her favorite seat. "Here ya go, Drew." She patted the seat next to her as Drew was about to breeze past.

"Oh. . .Dani. . .I thought you realized. . . I'll be eating lunch at Trevor's table from now on." Drew nervously chewed on the side of her fingernail. She didn't want to hurt Dani, but she was sure it was inevitable. "You're welcome to join us."

"I just didn't think. Of course you'll be eating with Trevor. . .I guess it just didn't click." Dani looked fine about what she was saying, but Drew knew her inside and out. Dani was crushed. It was a sad realization that she would be eating relatively alone from now on. Sure, there were other people who would be around, friends of theirs she could talk to, girls to joke around with while she ate her lunch. But the loss of the presence of the other half of her heart made the remaining half feel broken.

Drew pretended to believe that Dani was fine with it all and headed over to sit with Trevor. Somehow, though, her excitement had diminished and the sparkle was dimmed because she knew that she had disappointed her sister. Drew managed to put her guilt aside as soon as she saw how happy the group was to see her. She, a new freshman, was eating lunch at the table where all of the star football players and varsity cheerleaders ate. She beamed with pride while trying to maintain her composure so they wouldn't know how excited she actually was.

"Hey, there's my girl," Trevor said above the loud lunchroom noises.

"Hey, you. I'm famished. What's for lunch today?" Drew asked, sliding into the seat beside Trevor.

Sam informed her that the hot lunch was

beef tips and noodles but that she wouldn't eat something so fattening, so she was just having the salad option.

"Yeah, that's a good idea. I sure don't want those extra calories either." In reality, Drew would have loved the beef and noodles; it was one of her favorite hot lunches. But she surely didn't want the group to think she wasn't watching her weight. She went to the lunch counter and came back with a side salad and dinner roll, hoping it would tide her over until she got home that afternoon.

Lunch was a party of laughter and chatting. The time went too fast for Drew. While she did enjoy herself immensely, the whole thing was bittersweet as she watched her sister sit quietly across the lunchroom. Drew wondered for a moment if she had made a mistake. She didn't want to choose her new friends over her sister. But then again, she reasoned, she shouldn't be forced to. Her sister should want her to do the things that made her happy and to meet new people.

"Meet me after school outside the sports office?" Trevor whispered to Drew before they broke to head to their afternoon classes.

"I don't think I can stay long. I have to meet Dani right after school today, but I can't remember why. I could meet you for a few minutes, though," Drew offered.

"A few minutes is all I need." Trevor smiled suggestively, making Drew wonder what he was up to.

She laughed and said, "I can't figure you out half the time. But all right, I'll meet you there right after school for a few minutes." She waved at the rest of the group as they all headed off in their separate directions. She had hoped to break away with enough time to see Dani before class, but Dani was already gone. Drew sighed and hoped that she could make it up to her at home later.

The final bell rang, signaling the end of the school day. Drew hurriedly gathered her books and things and headed for her locker. She shoved everything in there—keeping the one book that she needed for homework—grabbed her purse, and hurried for the sports office, eager to find out why Trevor wanted to see her.

Walking down the corridor toward the sports office, Drew smiled and realized that she would be spending a lot of time in that corridor over the next four years. Spotting Trevor talking to his coach, Drew hung back for a moment, giving them space. As soon as he saw her, though, he broke away from his conversation, clapping the coach on the back, and headed over to her immediately. "I know you only have a couple of minutes, so let's not waste a moment's time."

"Sounds good to me, I think. Where are we going?"

"Follow me." He grabbed her hand and headed toward the exit that led to the football field. They walked quickly onto the field and then climbed into the bleachers.

After climbing all the way to the top of the bleachers, he pulled her down to the seat beside him. "Look out there." Trevor pointed to the empty football field. "Have you ever seen it like this?" When Drew shook her head no, he continued. "I love seeing it empty like this. It reminds me of how big it really is. It's amazing to me that it sits here lonely like this until we come and bring it to life. It really gets me charged up."

"Oh, I can see what you're saying. What a beautiful thought. You really can't get the feel of the place when it's full of people in the stands and players on the field. It's nice to sit back and get to know the personality of it when it's alone."

"That's exactly how I feel about it. It's alive."

Drew smiled and sighed as she looked around the empty field. She looked from one end of the field, through the bleachers on the other side, and past the goal posts on the other end of the field, around back to where they were seated. Once she had her fill of the sights, she looked at Trevor, only to realize that he was looking at her. Had he had been looking at her the whole time?

Trevor smiled at her and cupped her chin in his hand and leaned toward her. Here it came. Her first kiss. It was probably under the perfect circumstances; but she also wasn't really ready for it. Still, she wanted Trevor to kiss her, and she wouldn't dream of telling him not to.

As all of those thoughts sailed through her mind, he leaned in toward her lips. She should probably do her part and meet him halfway so that he wouldn't think she didn't want the kiss.

Palms sweating, cheeks on fire, she leaned toward Trevor. Their lips met in a soft, quick kiss. Just as quickly, they both backed away. She was thankful that it was over fast. It was all she could handle.

Flushed and breathless, they looked at each other for a moment and Drew began to giggle.

Trevor laughed and said, "You've really gotten to me, Drew Daniels. I never expected to get serious about someone this year."

"You've gotten to me, too. Believe me," Drew assured him. "I'm really glad, though."

Knowing that it was time for Drew to head home, they got up from their seats and retraced their steps back through the building. At the school's entrance, Trevor squeezed Drew's hand and said that he would see her tomorrow. She smiled and turned to walk in the direction of her house. Not riding the bus, like she sometimes did, would mean a long walk alone. Immediately she saw the spot where she normally met her sister.

With horror, Drew remembered that she had told Dani that she would meet her there after school so they could walk home together. She had never told Dani that she wouldn't be there.

With a backward glance over her shoulder at Trevor, she smiled and waved again, then headed quickly for home. Worried about how her sister was feeling, she jogged part of the way.

What a day. She had dropped the bomb on Dani that they wouldn't be eating lunch together anymore and then completely blew her off after school. Dani was probably at home, feeling very left out and lonely. Drew knew that's how she would feel if the roles were reversed.

But on the other hand, should Drew be stuck only doing what Dani wanted to do? Didn't Drew have the right to make new friends and have new experiences? She spent the remainder of the walk trying to convince herself, against nagging doubts, that she had done nothing wrong when it came to her treatment of Dani. She also hoped that Dani wasn't mad enough at her to tell Mom all that had been going on. Realizing that was a real risk, Drew promised herself that she would be much more careful in the future.

Tentatively walking into the house, Drew cautiously called out Dani's name. She wasn't sitting on the couch watching TV where Drew had expected she would be.

"Dani?" Drew called hesitantly and softly as she climbed the stairs toward their room. "We need to talk. . . . Dani? Dani?" Drew poked her head in every room, looking for her sister, but it was clear that she was nowhere to be found. Drew started to worry and considered calling Mom on her cell phone. Before she did anything, though, she needed to wash her makeup off.

Back in the family room, after scrubbing her face, Drew sat down on the couch to think things through. Where could Dani be? Why hadn't she come home? Or had she come home and left? Should Drew call one of their parents?

She walked into the kitchen to see if Dani's backpack was where she normally dropped it when she got home. No backpack, so Drew assumed that Dani hadn't come home at all yet. Where could she be?

Suddenly, the realization hit her. Today was the day of Dani's tryout for the debate team. They had been working with her to prepare for days. How could she have forgotten? Dani was going to be crushed, and her parents would likely be angry. Oh man, she really did it this time.

At about that time, Drew heard the garage door opening. Trying to look casual, she got a quick glass of milk and sat at the kitchen table. When they walked in, Drew said, "Hey, guys. How did it go? I'm so sorry I couldn't make it."

Dani wouldn't even look at Drew as she hurried out of the kitchen and went upstairs. But not before Drew noticed that Dani's eyes were bloodshot; she had been crying. The pain was evident in Dani's sad eyes. It broke Drew's heart when she realized how much Dani was hurting.

"Mom. . .I. . .what can I say? What can I do? I'm so sorry. I forgot to let Dani know that I wouldn't be able to meet her after school. It doesn't mean anything. I just had something come up for cheerleading that I needed to do." Drew felt bad about lying, but she didn't think she had a choice. She didn't want to hurt her sister even more with the truth.

"Drew, you need to talk to your sister. This isn't something I can fix for you. And next time something comes up like that, you need to call home and let someone know where you'll be and what time you'll be home. Okay?"

Drew agreed and apologized for the oversight; and then, eager to talk to Dani, she left the kitchen and went upstairs to find Dani crying softly on her bed.

"Dani, I'm so sorry. I'm sorry I couldn't be there, and I'm sorry that the tryout didn't go well."

"You *could* have been there, but you chose not to be. Don't think I didn't see you in the bleachers with Trevor. You picked him over me again. . . and on such an important day. You have no idea how much that hurt, still hurts actually."

"To be honest, Dani, I forgot about it for a little bit after school. It wasn't like I made a conscious choice to ignore you and your needs."

"Drew, this goes so much deeper than just forgetting me after school. It's about the fact that you are slowly pulling away from everything having anything to do with me, and it just doesn't seem to bother you one bit. You don't even miss me."

Dani's words cut like a knife. Drew knew that Dani was right, and she didn't know what to say to make her feel better.

"Dani, it's just that I don't believe that we, or I, can't have both. Why can't we have our relationship *and* I can have a boyfriend and a commitment to a sport? Why does being your sister mean that's all I can have?"

"No, Drew, you've got it all wrong. Loyalty is the issue here. It's not about having it all—you could have it all without even trying. Instead, you have chosen that other stuff over me and pushed me aside without any consideration of my feelings. It's not that you want 'both,' it's that you want me to step aside and let you do your own thing until you decide you need me again. The sad thing is, I'll do that. I'll be here—I'm not going anywhere. But I can't pretend it doesn't hurt."

Drew was speechless, but tears began to form in her eyes. She never wanted to hurt Dani like she had.

"I was worried when you didn't show up, so I went looking for you. I saw your first kiss. Funny, that was something that I thought we would discuss and share with each other. I thought we would squeal and jump up and down and run upstairs to our room where we could dissect every single detail. But at this point, Drew, I don't even want to know about it. That is what I had to think about the whole time I was trying out for the debate team, which is as important to me as your cheerleading is to you. By the way, what makes you think that my tryout went badly?"

Drew said, "I haven't seen you so sad in a long time, so I assumed that you didn't make the team."

"Oh, I made the team all right. It's the fact

that I couldn't share it with you that broke my heart." Dani abruptly stood and started to leave the room. On her way to the stairs, she turned and looked hard at Drew. "I sure hope you know what you're doing."

Chapter 10

WHAT THEY DON'T KNOW

Drew missed Dani. Sure, they still shared a room and walked to school together, but their relationship ended there all week. Drew was busy after school with long practices every day, so Dani walked home alone after her shorter debate team practices. During school, Drew spent every spare second with Trevor, so Dani hung out with other people. At lunchtime, Drew sat with Trevor and his friends, so Dani ate with her other friends across the room. It was a sad week for Dani, and even for Drew in many ways. But mostly, Drew was enjoying her life and missed only certain things—things that she was more than willing to sacrifice.

Fridays were always supercharged with energy because there was usually a football game that night. When it was an away game, the teams wore their white uniforms with red and gold accents to school on Friday. Home games were the best, though. The community turned out in support, and, together with hundreds of students, they showed their spirit in so many ways. When it was a home game, they wore the red uniforms with the white and gold accents to school that day. Drew loved wearing her uniform to school; it made her feel really important.

As Drew was putting her books into her locker, Trevor sneaked up behind her and put his arm around her neck and gave a playful squeeze.

"Hey, there, silly. How are you today?" She looked him up and down in approval and he did the same.

"You look great," they said to each other simultaneously and then laughed.

"Are we going to eat and party after the game tonight?"

"I hope so. I'll have to check with my parents."

Trevor rolled his eyes. "Come on, they need to get with the times and understand that you've got things to do." He laughed at his teasing, but Drew could also tell that he didn't like to be put off by such immature things as needing permission.

"Oh come on, you know how it is. They just have trouble letting go of their little girl. I'm sure you had a curfew when you were a freshman, too." Drew laughed good-naturedly.

"That's not really the point. You know, Drew, I'm not used to dating a freshman; I'm sort of past all of that needing permission stuff. I hope this isn't going to be a problem. I mean, I want to have my girl with me when I celebrate, not have to have her home and in bed by ten o'clock or some other crazy curfew."

Drew was slightly annoyed by his lack of understanding but didn't want to let him see that. "I'll do the best I can, Trevor. I hope I can work it out."

"Parents don't need to know everything. You don't have to say that you want to spend time with your boyfriend and that it's a date. Just tell them it's a school event and that everyone goes out after the game. Or even better, tell them you're spending the night at a friend's house. That way we can stay out later. You could stay at

Samantha's after our date."

"She hasn't invited me, though," Drew protested.

"Oh, don't worry about that at all. She does this all the time."

"Okay. I'll think about it. Don't worry about it, though. I'll figure it out. We'll definitely go out after the game."

"Good. That's my girl. I've got to run to class or I'll be late. See you!"

Drew smiled as he ran down the hall, dodging bodies along the way like any good quarterback would do. No matter how far away he got, Drew could still see his tall frame and broad shoulders above the crowd. Smiling and lost in thought, she finished collecting her books and went to class, thinking about how she would get permission to go out with the gang after the game.

"Drew! You're going to be late. Let's go!" Mom called up the stairs. Drew had rushed home from school to shower and get dressed in her uniform in preparation for their second home game. She was so excited about the game but also nervous about getting the permission she needed to go out afterward.

Skipping down the stairs, dark ponytail bouncing with each step, Drew said, "Here I come, Mom. Is everyone else ready?"

"Yep, we're all waiting. Let's go."

On the way there, Mom said, "After the game, I think we should all go out for ice cream to celebrate."

"Um, that's a good idea. . .but I sort of thought I would ask if I could make other plans." Drew hesitantly broached the subject of her "date."

"What were you hoping to do tonight, Drew?" Dad jumped in with concern.

"Oh, it's no big deal. It's just that the teams usually go out to The Grill after games, and it's such a fun thing to be a part of. I was hoping that I'd be able to make that a part of my game-night ritual—at least for home games."

"Well, let us think about it, and we'll talk about it after the game," Mrs. Daniels suggested.

"Okay. That's fine." Drew didn't want to argue, because she knew it wouldn't do any good; but she really had hoped to have this worked out before the game. No matter. . .she'd figure it out after the game. Maybe spending the night at Sam's would be the best idea. Ignoring feelings of guilt, she tried to refocus her thoughts on the game.

The game was exciting. The crowd was wild and the players were doing great. By halftime, they were winning by fourteen points. It was dark by that time, and the stadium lights gave the whole atmosphere a completely different feel. The halftime show was perfectly executed and generated enough buzz in the crowd to get the team through the second half. Drew loved every minute of it. After the performance, there were some other things taking place on the field, so Trevor and Drew had a few moments to chat.

"Hey, you. You looked really hot out there," Trevor said with a big grin on his face.

"You aren't so bad yourself." Drew winked at him.

"I wanted to tell you, instead of going to The Grill, there's a huge party tonight. It happens to be at Sam's house. She has a big pool and a field behind her house where we'll have a bonfire. We'll go there instead. It's going to be awesome. And Sam said there was no problem with you spending the night. She even said that her older sister would vouch for you if your mom wanted to talk to her *mom*."

"That sounds terrific." Drew's stomach turned at the lies she would have to tell in order to make the date with Trevor. Not to mention the trouble she would get into if she got caught. But the thought of not going was just as upsetting to her. She only had the second half of the game to decide what she was going to do.

It was an agonizing hour and a half as Drew's mind filled with all of the reasons why she didn't want to do it, countered with tons of reasons why she did. She dreaded the thought of lying to her parents and also felt a nudge in her spirit that reminded her of how much this went against what God would want her to do.

She wanted to be a part of all that was going on, and she really believed that she should be allowed to go. She rationalized that her parents would let her spend the night at Samantha's, so that wasn't a lie. And it wasn't really up to her who else Sam invited to her house. . .then again, Drew's mom and dad would never let her go if they knew there wouldn't be an adult there. If she got caught lying and breaking so many rules, she would surely be grounded for a long time and not be given permission for things like this for a long, long time. However, if she didn't get caught and it worked out great, she would have catapulted her popularity and proven to Trevor that she was fun to be with and willing to make spending time with him a priority, no matter what.

Drew couldn't remember a time when she was so torn over a decision. She had finally gotten to the point where she just wasn't going to go. After all, nothing good should be that difficult. Just as her thoughts had begun to swing in that direction, Trevor came jogging off the field and went in for a drink of water.

He stopped for a minute to talk to Drew and told her, "Drew, you're the cutest thing I've ever seen." He chuckled and continued, "You completely distract me out there. I really hope you are able to come with me tonight. I just want you by my side. I like being close to you."

His words melted her and made her tremble. No one had ever talked to her like that, and it was a heady feeling to be liked so much by the coolest boy in school. She was more confused than ever after that. Wishing she had more time to decide, she went out onto the field to lead the squad in cheering the team on to the end of the game and another victory. After the celebratory lap around the field and the handshakes and high fives with the other team, it was her moment of truth.

The time has come for you to make your decision. Think long and hard about what you would really do if you were faced with the decision that Drew is facing. It's easy to say that you'd make the right choice. But are you sure that you could stand up to your boyfriend and face his rejection? Once your decision is made, turn to the corresponding page in this book to see how it turns out for Drew—and for you.

Turn to page 315 if Drew is able to stand up to Trevor by not going to the party.

Turn to page 344 if Drew is unable to avoid the temptation and gives in to what Trevor wants her to do.

The next three chapters tell the story of what happened to Drew when she decided to do what she knew was right.

Chapter 11

GONE TOO FAR

Drew knew what she had to do. She was going to have to tell her friends that she couldn't lie and go to the party and that she'd be going home with her family. She knew that she was risking her reputation among her new friends and especially with Trevor. She feared that he would think she was too immature to continue dating after this, or that his feelings would be hurt.

But regardless of what happened, she couldn't bring herself to blatantly lie to her parents, go to a party that they never would have allowed her to go to, spend time with a boy until very late into the night, and stay the night at a girl's house whose parents were out of town. Doing those things would destroy all trust that her parents had in her, and she knew it. She would face so much trouble that she wouldn't be able to spend time with Trevor or her new friends anyway, and using such poor judgment would keep her from dating forever, probably.

Decision made, she went to tell Trevor. She found him talking to one of his teammates. They were slapping each other on the back and celebrating a fantastic game. Drew cleared her throat to get their attention.

Trevor turned to see her and said, "Hey, there's my girl." He walked over to her and gave her a little squeeze and a quick kiss on the cheek.

"Great game, Trevor. You did an awesome job out there."

Trevor beamed with the praise. "You about ready to go? We need to stop and pick up a few things on the way to the party," Trevor said, assuming that she was going.

"Um. . .I need to talk to you about that. I'm not going to be able to go," Drew hesitantly said, biting her lip. "I just can't do it—too many lies and the risk of too much trouble. It's just too much."

Trevor didn't look happy. At first he looked disappointed, but that look quickly turned to anger. "Do you have any idea what you're saying? You're telling me that after a game like this, you're going to leave me dateless and alone at the party of the year? I need you there. You're my girl. You're supposed to be there with me, by my side."

"I can't help it, Trevor. I want to go—really, I do. But I don't want to lie to my parents. And if I were to get caught, we'd never see each other again anyway."

Trevor groaned. "This is what I get for dating a freshman."

"You know, you could be a little more supportive. I'm just trying to do the right thing," Drew tried to explain.

"No Drew, it's you who could be more supportive." Trevor shook his head in disgust. "So is your mind made up? Is that it? You're not going to go no matter what I say?"

"I'm not going to go." Drew hung her head as she said the words, knowing that she was likely sealing the deal on the end of their relationship.

"Then I guess you'd better go find your family. It's past your bedtime, and I have to go," Trevor answered sarcastically.

How dare he? Drew took a deep breath to

quell the sob that rose in her throat. She was devastated by his reaction but also miffed that he cared so little about her that he would be angry at her for trying to do the right thing. "Thanks for the support and understanding, Trevor. You've made this all about you, which tells me that you don't really care about me anyway. You only care about how I make you look. I guess I made the right decision. Have fun." With that, she turned and walked away with her head down, hoping he wouldn't see the tears forming in her eyes.

She noticed her parents standing by the car, waiting like they had after the previous game. Trying to compose herself before she got to the car, she stopped and turned to say something to someone passing by. As she did so, she wiped at her eyes and tried to find her smile again. When she turned to face her parents, she looked almost normal. She knew that they could probably see right through her attempts at normalcy but hoped they wouldn't ask about it.

"I changed my mind. I'm going to go with you guys. Is that ice cream offer still good?"

"Of course, dear. It'll be fun. Let's go," Dad said with a big grin.

Mrs. Daniels looked hard at Drew, but said nothing.

The girls piled into the backseat, and Dad backed the car out of the parking space. Drew felt Dani staring at her, trying to figure out what was going on. She refused to look her in the eye, because Dani would immediately be able to see through her shaky expression of happiness and see that there was sorrow beneath it—and it would probably make Drew cry for real.

As they pulled away from the school, Drew looked out the window and saw Trevor and a bunch of his teammates and some cheerleaders at the end of the parking lot horsing around. It looked like they were getting ready to pack up some cars and head out. They were laughing and having a great time. Trevor sure didn't look sad at all.

Then she saw the unthinkable. Trevor put his arm across the shoulders of one of the varsity cheerleaders. Drew couldn't see who it was exactly, because she was looking at the girl's back, and, in her cheerleading uniform, she looked just like every other cheerleader from the back. Trevor gave her a quick squeeze and started jogging back over to the sports office, presumably to get his things. He sure looked happy, like he didn't have a care in the world. No one would have ever guessed that he was a guy who had supposedly been crushed by a girlfriend he had proclaimed to like so very much that same evening. She felt sorry for the unsuspecting cheerleader who was just happy to have his attention—like Drew had been.

Drew realized that the car was too quiet, and if she didn't do something, they were going to start questioning her. She was in no mood or state of mind to answer questions about the evening. "So, where are we going? We haven't been out for ice cream in forever." She tried to sound energetic and positive.

"I was just wondering about that," Dad said. "Should we go somewhere that we can get a burger before we have ice cream? I think everyone is hungry."

"Sounds good to me," Dani spoke up from the backseat.

"Me, too." Drew tried to sound enthusiastic.

After the Danielses were seated and the waitress took their order for burgers, fries, and chocolate milkshakes all around, Mom looked at

Drew and asked, "Okay, what gives? Something happened tonight. You look so sad and disappointed." She waited for Drew to protest that everything was fine, but instead, she could see that Drew was really considering her words carefully.

Finally, Drew couldn't hold back any longer. She let the tears flow and spilled her emotions and the entire story onto the table. She told her family every detail, even the part about sneaking a ride home with Trevor and the kiss in the bleachers. She spared no detail. Not only was she tired of living what she felt was a lie and being so distant from her family, but she also didn't think it really mattered if she got grounded or into some kind of trouble, because she really had nowhere to go now anyway. Plus, it was time for her to get back to being the person she really was deep down.

Finishing the story by recounting the vision of Trevor with his arm around another girl on the way out of the parking lot that night, Drew dried her eyes with resolve not to cry over him anymore. He didn't care about her needs and wants and was willing to pressure her to do things that made her very uncomfortable. Drew knew that she was better off without him, but dreams die hard, and her mom knew that.

Just as Drew was finishing her story, the waitress brought the food. Drew dived into her burger with a vengeance, feeding her body and nursing her broken heart. Everyone at the table took a few moments to begin to eat and also to let Drew's words sink in.

Dani remained quiet, afraid to break the moment and wanting Drew to continue to come to her new realizations. She was so very happy that Drew had made the right decision, and it really sounded like she had grown through the experience. She hoped that her parents wouldn't be too hard on her.

"Drew. . .there are a lot of things I'd like to say. Are you ready for me to respond, or do you need more time?" Mom asked.

"Go ahead, Mom. But I pretty much already know what you're going to say."

"Oh? Try me. What am I about to say?"

"You're going to tell me how mad you are at me about the after-game thing last week. You're going to tell me that I'm way too young to have a boyfriend, and that I proved it by not telling you all about it. You're going to tell me that I shouldn't have kissed him. I'm going to be punished for sneaking around and for doing things that I knew you wouldn't approve of like the makeup and the clothes. Basically, you're going to tell me how disappointed you are in me. Right?"

"Well, sweetie, I'm speaking for myself, and your dad may feel much differently, but that is about the exact opposite of what I want to say to you."

"Huh? What do you mean?"

"I have never, ever been more proud of you, Drew. You faced some very grown-up things in a few short weeks. And you were tempted by the glitter and sparkle of adult life and you made some decisions that I wouldn't have approved of, that's for sure. But Drew, look at the result. You have surprised me by the fact that when push came to shove, you gave up all of the things that you wanted so badly and chose what was right. You lost a lot tonight, by your own choice. But by doing that, you gained even more."

"I think that your mom is trying to say that you've grown through this," Dad explained. "And you've shown us clearly what type of young lady you really are. We really like what we see."

Drew was in tears again—this time, tears of relief. She was so blown away by her parents' reaction that she didn't know what to say. She thought of Pastor Michaels's words. "Remember last week when Pastor Michaels talked about how when we impose our own will over God's plan, that it's like saying, 'I've got everything under control'? And that is a pride issue. . .you know. . .to think that we know more than God." At her parents' nod, she continued. "Well, I said those words several times this week: 'I've got it all under control.' Turns out, I didn't. Pastor Michaels was right. And you guys, my parents, kind of act as a stand-in for God. So, your rules—or what you want for me and from me—are just an extension of God's will. Right?"

Flabbergasted, Mom said, "You're very right."

"Well, I guess what I want is to live for God and walk according to His will. That means I don't have everything under control. . .you guys do. I'm not saying I'll be perfect, but I guess I just want something different—I want to do it right. Does that make sense?"

"Perfect sense."

"For the record," Dani jumped in, "I totally agree with you, Drew. And I'm so glad to hear you saying this. I was really getting worried about you. I guess I should have known that, as smart as you are, you'd come around."

"Thanks, sis. Can you ever forgive me for the way I've treated you this past month?"

"Of course I can. I love you. . .it's forgiven. Now, let's just move on. I'd like us to commit to supporting each other in doing the right thing from now on. I feel like I should have tried a lot harder to keep you on the straight and narrow. I guess I was too hurt and bitter. I'm sorry for that."

"Dani, you have nothing to be sorry for. You're the best sister a girl could ever hope for. And I love you, too."

"Drew, one thing you may not have thought of yet," Mom hesitated, "and we can talk more about this throughout the weekend, but it's going to be tough to go back to school on Monday. We need to have a plan for you and also to surround you in prayer that you'll be able to stand your ground no matter what."

"Great point, Mom. Monday seems so far

away right now, though. "This is what I care most about." She spread her hands to gesture to her family at the table. She was home.

Chapter 12

REAL FRIENDS

After staying in and laying low on Sunday, except for attending church, Drew felt mentally and emotionally prepared for school. Dani was so good to encourage her and promise support. Really, though, Drew had done nothing wrong, and people broke up all the time. She hoped her new friends wouldn't abandon her, too. She was realistic enough to know that Trevor was their golden boy, so it would be up to him and what he said about her that would determine how everyone else responded to her. Her best bet, she knew, was to look confident and happy when she went to school. Hanging her head and hiding from the group would only fuel the impression of her immaturity.

She rose early and carefully dressed for school. Wanting to look great, but not like she was trying too hard, Drew selected her favorite pair of jeans and one of the new tops that she bought for herself. It was important to keep being herself. She did promise her mom that she wouldn't sneak makeup anymore, though. As part of that deal, her parents had agreed to a few new things that she was allowed to wear. She could now wear light lipstick or colored lip gloss, soft blush on her cheeks, and mascara to lengthen her eyelashes. Still forbidden were any colors of eye shadow, eyeliner, or lip liner. So Drew carefully applied her makeup within the new guidelines. One last look in the mirror reflected success. She really had to admit that the look was much softer and prettier than the garish effect of lots of makeup. Her mom had been right about that one.

Threading her favorite belt through the frayed loops on her jeans and securing the buckle as she went downstairs to the kitchen, Drew realized that her stomach was too upset to eat. Her mom must have known that she'd feel that way, because all that she handed to Drew when she arrived in the kitchen was a piece of buttered toast. Drew, gratefully took the plate and sat down to eat.

The time passed quickly, and there were no more reasons to stall. Drew and Dani got ready to catch the bus. Taking a shuddering deep breath, Drew grabbed her things and prepared to leave the house.

With her hand on the door, Mom asked if she could pray for her.

"Of course, Mom. Thanks."

"Father, please be with Drew today. Give her peace and wisdom as she faces this difficult situation. Let her find favor with the students whom You have selected to be her friends, and let her peacefully accept that some will not turn out to be true friends. Help her be strong and stand for You. Keep both of my girls safe at school today and make them strong and powerful examples of You and Your love. Amen."

"Thanks, Mom." Drew hugged her mom and started to leave.

"I love you both."

"We love you, too, Mom," Drew and Dani answered simultaneously.

Arriving at school, Drew took a deep breath as the bus squealed to a stop. Dani reached over and took her sister's hand. "It's going to be okay. The first hour is the hardest. After that, it just gets easier. I promise."

"You're the best, Dani. I am so glad you're my sister and my best friend." She took another deep breath, fluffed her hair, squared her shoulders, and went down the steps of the bus. "Here we go."

The girls walked into the school with their heads held high. They talked and laughed and acted as though they didn't have a care in the world. They made it all the way to their lockers without bumping into anyone upsetting to Drew. Students still gave her the usual comments about her clothes and the halls were peppered with the usual shouts of "Hi, Drew" all along the way. She hadn't lost her status yet. But Drew wondered if that was just because news hadn't traveled that fast.

"You're here? I can't believe you're okay." Cara, their longtime friend, came running up to the girls.

"Yeah, I guess you heard, huh? Well, there was no way that my mom was going to let me skip school just because I was sad about breaking up with Trevor."

"Breaking up with Trevor? That's not what I'm talking about at all. Didn't you hear what happened?" Cara was breathless with excitement.

"I guess I haven't heard. What happened?" Drew asked Cara just to be polite but wasn't really interested in anyone else's gossip; she had enough of her own to deal with.

"Well. . ." Cara excitedly started her story. "I guess there was a big party at Samantha's house after the game. Anyway, there was drinking, some drugs, and loud music. Neighbors called the cops, and a bunch of kids got arrested for the alcohol, drugs, and for disturbing the peace. Sam's older sister also got in trouble for providing alcohol to minors. I guess some of the guys from school even had fake IDs. It's a big mess."

"Oh my goodness, I can't believe it. I was supposed to be at that party. I chose not to go because I didn't want to lie to my parents, and that's why Trevor dumped me."

"What a jerk! Well, he got what was coming to him."

"No, I don't wish that kind of trouble on anyone. I feel really bad that they all went through that this weekend. I had no idea. Here

I was all wrapped up in my own little drama, which was nothing in comparison. I wonder if they'll be at school."

"I saw Sam already but not Trevor, and I don't know who else got into trouble. I'm sure we'll find out more as the day goes on. But I'm really sorry, Drew. I'm sure you must have been really hurt."

"Yeah, it's been a tough weekend. But Dani and I have had a chance to spend a lot of time together, and I've missed that. So something good came of it all."

"Hang in there today, Drew. Your real friends will show what they're made of. The rest don't really matter anyway." Cara and Dani shared a first-period class, so they left together after making sure that Drew would be okay.

Drew finished putting her books in her locker and then turned to go to class. As she turned, she bumped into Samantha. Sam's eyes looked haunted and scared. Drew immediately realized that the weekend had taken a big toll on her. Sam looked at Drew in disgust and walked the other way. Drew gave herself a pep talk. Sam's reaction really had nothing to do with her. She was just taking out her own fears on whoever was near.

It meant nothing, and Drew decided not to let it bother her. One down, one more to go. Trevor was the only other one she was nervous about seeing. The rest would work itself out.

Morning classes passed by too quickly, and it was time for the dreaded lunch hour. Part of her felt that it would be best to go to Trevor's table and just sit down to have lunch there. She hadn't actually been uninvited. But she didn't want to suffer the humiliation of being publicly shunned. Or, on the off chance that he was happy to see her, Drew didn't want to send the message that his treatment of her was okay. So her plan was to sit with Dani, Cara, and their other friends at lunch. Drew even brought her lunch to school that day so that she wouldn't have to walk past Trevor and his friends to get a hot lunch.

Sliding into a seat at the end of the table, Drew kept her back to Trevor's table. She realized that she hadn't seen him all day, though. Suddenly she wondered if he were even at school that day. Ah, there he was. Across the lunchroom, she saw his broad shoulders towering above the other students. Sadly, she slumped into her seat and made sure not to look back. She needed a few moments to regain her resolve.

The girls chatted their way through lunch with all sorts of small talk. Drew contributed a lot of grunts and groans. Finally she realized what a drag she had been and apologized. "I'm really sorry for being in such a slump. I guess this is harder than I thought it would be."

"It's totally understandable—" Cara started to say but stopped short.

Samantha approached the table and wanted to talk to Drew. The other girls scooted down a little bit to make room for Sam, but they weren't about to leave Drew alone with her yet.

"So, Drew, did you have fun on Friday night? Did you get to go home with Mommy and Daddy and get a special treat for being such a good girl?"

"What's your problem, Sam?" Drew straightened her back, not willing to let Sam's anger get to her. "Didn't you have a curfew or rules when you were in the ninth grade? Eh, maybe you didn't. Maybe your parents let you do whatever you wanted. I guess that didn't pay off too well for you, according to rumors. Looks like I made the right choice. Sure wish you guys could support that."

"Support that? You want me to support

your abandonment and betrayal of us, your supposed friends?" Sam looked truly shocked at the suggestion, and it just made Drew realize that they weren't operating with the same moral compass.

"Yes, I do think you should have supported me—if you were truly my friend, that is. A true friend wouldn't want to put her friend in a situation that was uncomfortable. A true friend would back up the tough decisions and allow for the differences between us. A false friend only wants what she wants for herself and has no thought for others."

"Are you suggesting that I fit your description of a false friend?" Sam was getting angry.

"Well, Sam, think about it. It's all I know of you. During our short friendship, everything was great as long as I was going along with what you guys wanted. As soon as I took a stand as an individual person, you took it personally and got angry with me, even to the point of dropping me as your friend. I don't really want to discuss it any further. I can't convince you, and I don't have to. Just think about what I said. I have to get to class."

Chapter 13

LESSONS,
THE HARD WAY

As the week went on, Drew learned more details about last Friday night. The gang all showed up at Sam's house after the game. Her parents were out of town, so the closest thing to an adult was her twenty-two-year-old sister. They started a bonfire in the fire pit, and Sam's sister went to buy them a bunch of beer. Apparently Trevor even used a fake ID to buy beer, too. Sam, Trevor, and the rest of them stood around the bonfire, drinking beer for hours. Eventually, things got a little crazy. Someone brought out some drugs to pass around, and most of them sampled it. Kids were splashing in the pool and screaming at all hours. Finally, at about one in the morning, one of the neighbors apparently had enough with the noise and constant commotion—maybe they even suspected the kids had drugs—and called the police.

Three police cars arrived with lights and sirens blaring. They pulled into the driveway sideways to block in all of the cars. They went around to the backyard immediately, called a stop to the party, and herded all of the students onto the back porch. Several were let go when it was determined that they hadn't been drinking. Most of the others were told to walk in a straight line and touch their fingers to their noses. Some were too drunk to even be tested. All of those who were detained were eventually read their rights and placed in a squad car to be taken to the police station.

The majority of the teens were charged with the consumption of alcohol as a minor. Drew was told that a charge like that would mean a fine and some community service, most likely. Many of them, including Sam and Trevor, were charged with that plus a charge related to the drug use; and Trevor even got in trouble for buying alcohol with a fake ID. It sounded like Trevor was in a lot of trouble. Kids were even talking about him being sent away somewhere. And a couple of others, including Sam's sister, were charged as adults with crimes related to supplying alcohol to minors. All of them were taken to the police station, formally charged, fingerprinted, and locked up until their parents could be reached. They each had to call their parents to come and pick them up from the police station—what a tough call that must have been. Sam and her sister actually had to stay in jail overnight until their parents could get back into town to pick them up.

It was a horrible mess, and it broke Drew's heart that her friends—real friends or not—had to go through something like that. Even though things turned out badly with Trevor, Drew still cared about him and would never want to see him hurting like this. She couldn't even imagine how he must have felt there in the police station while waiting for his parents to arrive. And she had no idea what the legal situation would be. She hoped that, no matter what happened, this would be something that the Lord would use to wake him up.

It was a strange week, because Drew knew they were ignoring her. She supposed that being ignored was better than being ridiculed or called out for her decisions. By Thursday, Drew had basically let go and realized that they weren't going to come around. So she just stuck with her sister and her real friends and enjoyed her cheerleading squad. She really had no need for those older kids, anyway. She had a lot more in common with the others.

On Thursday, just as they were finishing up their lunches, Dani said, "Um, Drew. . . Trevor's on his way over here. Be strong."

Drew panicked for a minute. She wasn't prepared to talk to him, because she didn't know what he was going to say to her. She could handle being ignored, but to be confronted by Trevor would be very difficult for her. She said a quick prayer for peace and wisdom and hoped that she'd be strong.

"Hey, Drew. Mind if I sit down for a minute?" Trevor asked when he got to the table.

The other girls took the cue and left the table, giving them a moment alone. As she squeezed past her sister, Dani gave Drew's shoulder a little squeeze for strength.

"Sure, it's a free country." Drew motioned to an empty seat, not quite being rude, but not being too gracious, either.

Trevor was quiet for a minute. He fidgeted in his seat. "First, I just wanted to apologize for how I acted. I never should have pressured you like I did, and I feel horrible for being such a jerk."

"Thank you for saying that. I appreciate it." Drew wasn't about to gush or make it easy for him, but she had no reason to make it any more difficult than it already was.

"You must have really felt bad after the way I treated you."

Drew nodded and wiped at a tear that she had tried unsuccessfully to will away.

"The thing is, I don't know what came over me. It's not like me to be so insensitive."

"Power." Drew barely whispered the one word that came to her mind.

"Did you say 'power'? What do you mean?"

"I mean that the power got to you. You were having a pretty exciting few weeks; and the power of getting exactly what you wanted was getting to you, and you demanded your way from everyone, even from me."

Trevor thought for a moment. "I guess you're right. Anyway, I'm sorry. You did the right thing. . . . Well. . .obviously, by the way things turned out, you did the right thing."

"Thank you. I know I did. It was difficult, though."

"I'm sure it was. You're much stronger than I am." Trevor hung his head, overcome with regret and sadness. "Is there anything I can do to patch things up between us? I'd really like to keep seeing you, Drew."

"Trevor, I like you, I really do. But I think I've learned that there are big differences between kids our ages, and I'm just not ready to make that leap. I want to enjoy the place I am right now and not rush things. Plus, my personal opinion is that you need some time to focus on what you want for yourself. I don't want to be a distraction in that process. You have a lot on your plate, a lot that you're facing. I think you should face first things first—and not worry about a girlfriend right now. Trevor, maybe it's time you stop sleeping in on Sunday mornings and start going to church. That's where you'll find the answers you're looking for."

"I'll think about it. And I understand. I'm not giving up, though. Maybe in a few months, when all of this is behind us, maybe you'll want to give it another try then."

"We never know what the future may hold; but at this point, I have no plans to get involved with someone this year. I've learned my lesson."

"Well, then, good for you. I hope I've learned some lessons, too."

"Me, too, Trevor. Me, too."

"Can we still be friends?" Trevor asked hopefully.

"Of course we can be friends. But I'm sticking with my best friends for the most part. I'll see you around, and we can be nice to each other; but I don't see us hanging out like we once did. It's okay, though. It's part of the process. You see, I made some mistakes in all of this, too. I was a really bad friend and sister during my supposed climb to the top, and I won't be letting that happen again. I'm sure you can understand."

"I've learned a lot from you, Drew. I hope you find all of the happiness you deserve."

They parted for class. Drew felt strong and incredibly relieved. God answered her prayers and gave her strength she didn't think she had—and also gave her a way out when there seemed to be no way. As she walked to class, she quietly thanked Him for being with her and giving her the words to say. She also prayed for Trevor and the difficult situation he was in legally. She prayed for mercy for him and that he would learn about life and love through this situation. She then thanked the Lord for guiding her through the tough choices she had faced and asked Him to keep leading her every step of the way. For the first time that week, she felt happy. She walked to class with her head held high and with a smile on her face, confident that God had everything under control.

The next three chapters tell the story of what happened to Drew when she decided to give in to the pressure by doing what her friends were asking her to do.

Chapter 11

PARTY TIME

"I'm definitely going to go. You're sure it's okay to spend the night at Sam's?"

"Oh, yeah. She told me it was fine," Trevor assured Drew.

"All right, then I'm going to go tell my parents. I'll be right back." Drew ran off to find her family waiting patiently by the car.

"So, what's your plan, Drew?" Mom asked when Drew ran up. "By the way," she threw in before Drew could answer about her plans, "you looked fantastic out there again. You do such a great job." Dad and Dani agreed.

"Thanks, guys. I'm so glad you came." Drew was happy to hear their comments but still nervous, because she knew she was about to lie to them. "Well, about tonight, I'd like to go with the squad to eat and then with the other girls over to Sam's house to spend the night. I have clothes and stuff already in my gym bag from earlier today. And I'll just have someone drop me off sometime in the morning." She left out the fact that it wouldn't be just girls at Sam's and that Sam's parents were out of town.

"That sounds fine. Her parents will be home, right?"

"Of course, Mom. Do you want the number?"

"Well, let me have the number in case of an emergency, but I trust you."

Drew gave her Sam's phone number, kissed her parents, said good-bye to Dani, who had been strangely quiet, and ran off to join her friends. When she got to Trevor's side, she said, "It's all set. I do need to tell Sam to make sure her sister knows that my mom might call. She probably won't, but just in case something happens, I want her to be prepared."

"I already told her all about that. So it's all set?" Trevor flashed a huge grin. "Excellent. Let's go. We have to stop at the store on the way." He opened the passenger door for her and, like a perfect gentleman, helped her fasten her seat belt.

"Why don't you wait here?" Trevor suggested when they arrived at the grocery store.

"Okay, if you want me to." Drew found that odd but figured he was just in a big hurry to get to the party.

Drew sat in the car, looking through Trevor's CDs for about fifteen minutes. She was just about to get out of the car to go look for him when she saw him pushing a full cart toward the car. He went straight to the trunk and loaded it up, got in the car, and they left for the party. It was about a fifteen-minute drive to Sam's house, but it flew by, because Trevor held Drew's hand the whole way there.

When they arrived at the party, the bonfire was already blazing and people were milling around Samantha's big backyard. A few people were swimming, even though it was a bit chilly. Drew surveyed the yard and saw at least fifty people there already, but many were clearly not in high school anymore as evidenced by the beer cans they were holding.

Sam came running up to Trevor and Drew. "Hey, guys. Glad you're here." Turning her attention to Trevor, she asked, "Did you get it?"

He answered, "Yep. It's in the trunk. I'll

unload it in a few minutes."

"Oh, it's okay. I'll help you. We can get it now," Drew offered.

Laughing, Trevor said, "Okay, you asked for it." He popped the trunk open with the remote on his key ring, and they walked around to the back.

Drew gasped when she saw the contents of the trunk. There were two or three bags full of chips and snacks right next to three cases of beer.

"How did you buy that?" Drew was shocked and afraid when she realized what kind of party this was going to be.

"It's called a fake ID, my dear." Trevor laughed. "Welcome to high school and the party of the year. Grab a bag and let's go."

Drew grabbed the bags of chips; she wasn't sure that she wanted anything to do with the beer. Walking into the house with the food, Drew was shocked to see kids she knew from school smoking cigarettes and drinking. She had heard about parties like this but had no idea this kind of thing actually went on in her school.

Trevor immediately popped the top off of a beer and took a big drink, as did Samantha. Drew just stared at them for a second. It surprised her that they could drink the beer so fast; it meant that this probably wasn't the first time. They offered her a beer and she declined. It was too much for her, but they laughed.

Samantha said, "If you want to run with the big kids, you need to act like one." They both continued to laugh but didn't pressure her anymore.

Trevor and Drew walked through the party—Drew with her can of soda and Trevor with his beer—stopping to talk to little groups of people. Eventually they all wound up out by the fire. Cans of beer were tossed around, making sure that no one was left empty-handed. Spirits were high; the party was in full swing.

Drew asked Trevor what time it was and how long he would be able to stay. "I'm just concerned about you driving home after drinking," she explained.

"Oh, don't worry about that, sweet thing." Trevor grinned and put his arm around her. "I'm not going anywhere tonight. I wouldn't leave you alone in this strange place. What kind of boyfriend would I be if I did that?"

Drew was so torn. She was happy to be there.

It made her feel so mature and part of the in crowd. But to get there that night, she had told no fewer than three big lies. She had broken some very important rules. She was sleeping over at a house where there were no adults. The sleepover was turning out to be boys and girls, including her boyfriend. She was also being offered alcohol and hanging out with kids who were drinking. Her own boyfriend even used a fake ID to buy beer. Even the fact that he was her "boyfriend" would have upset her parents.

As she attempted to sort through some of those truths, she started to smell something funny. It was like nothing she had ever smelled before, and she was pretty sure she didn't want to know what it was. She looked around the circle and saw kids smoking stuff that didn't look like regular cigarettes. Drugs! Someone had brought drugs to the party.

Drew stood and contemplated her situation for a few moments. She could go home. But if she called home, she would be in big trouble. Perhaps her best bet was to hope that nothing happened and that she didn't get caught. Tomorrow, it would all be over and she could go back to normal life, she hoped. But since she was there and had decided not to leave, and since she had decided not to let herself get in this predicament again, she thought it might be a good idea to take her opportunity to try some things that she may not have a chance to do again.

So in the next hour, she took a few puffs of Trevor's cigarette; she drank a beer, plus a few sips of a different kind of drink that Trevor had; and, with her judgment even more skewed by the alcohol, she actually allowed herself to be convinced to try the drugs that were being passed around.

She really didn't like how she was starting to feel—kind of fuzzy and like she was in slow motion—but after a while she started to get used to it and went for more beer. She really didn't want to get out of control, but she did want to have fun. So this is what it meant to party? It felt great to Drew. . .like second nature. She looked at her watch and was shocked to see that it was one in the morning. The time was going so fast, and Drew didn't want the night to end.

Trevor came up behind her, put his arms around her, and squeezed. "How's my girl doing? You having a good time?"

"Mmm-hmm," Drew murmured as she settled the back of her head against his broad chest. She liked the way it felt to be held, and for a minute she forgot where she was. He turned her around to face him and leaned in for a kiss. It was a much softer and longer kiss than the one they shared in the bleachers. It felt much more grown-up, and in no way did it make her giggle. Drew hoped that the moment would never stop.

Trevor pulled away slightly and said, "I like kissing you."

"Mmm, I like to be kissed." She smiled and kissed him again.

"Here," Trevor said as the pot came around through the group and back to them. He offered her some. She tried to decline, but Trevor teased her a bit and convinced her to have some more. "You can't really know how you'll feel until you try it for real. That one hit you took earlier just isn't enough to get the full effect."

Drew took it out of his hands and put it to her lips and lightly inhaled.

"Oh, no, that's not how you do it. Watch." Trevor demonstrated for her and then put it to her lips once more.

As Drew inhaled, she wondered why he

wanted her to smoke it so badly. She let the thought pass, though, and began to really feel the effects.

Trevor leaned in for another kiss, and this time, neither of them pulled away. Drew became a bit afraid that she'd never want this to stop, so she pulled away. "Let's go inside and get a snack. I'm starving."

"Okay, but you're not getting off that easily. We'll pick that up again a little later, maybe when we're alone."

Drew was afraid to consider what that might mean. But it didn't matter yet. The party was in full swing and some people were still arriving. She reminded herself that she was a smart girl and that she had everything under control.

Chapter 12

JUST NOT RIGHT

Back at home, Mom and Dad tried to relax and watch some TV before bed. But something was just not sitting right with them. They were uneasy about some of the things that Drew had said and some of the signals they read from her, but they had a difficult time deciding what it was that made them so uneasy.

"She was nervous," Mom said. "She was nervous and fidgety when she was talking to us. Do you think that's what is bugging us?"

"That could be it. You know, I've been thinking. . . " Dad hesitated. "I don't want to ask Dani to betray Drew, but maybe she knows something."

"We could talk to her. Or I could always try

calling Samantha's mom."

"That's a good idea. Do that first, and then, if we still need to, we can talk to Dani."

Mom dialed the phone and waited for someone to pick up. Finally someone answered, but the background noise was so loud that she could barely hear the person on the other end of the line.

Casting a nervous glance at her husband, Mom said, "I'm looking for Samantha's mom. Is she available?"

"No lady, she's out of town," the boy slurred and then hung up.

Mom sat and stared at the phone in her hand like it was a snake. After recounting the brief conversation to her husband, they were both so concerned that Mom immediately went upstairs to wake Dani up and ask her to join them in the family room.

Dani came down the stairs, sleepily rubbing her eyes. When she realized what they were asking her, she struggled over what to tell her parents. She wasn't willing to lie, but she really wanted to protect her sister as much as she could.

"Danielle,"—it was never a good thing when Dad used her full name—"if you know anything about where your sister is and what she might be doing, we need to know. It seems as though there is a lot more to the story than we were told, and we're concerned that she could be getting into some trouble. This is definitely not the time to try to protect your sister from getting caught. She could be facing much greater dangers than that."

Dani realized that this situation was much bigger than just wanting to protect her sister. Her love for Drew meant that she needed to help her parents help her sister. She wound up telling them everything she knew, starting with the first time Drew got a ride home from Trevor, and about the kiss in the bleachers, to what she had heard about this party around school. She told them that there was no adult there and that there was to be alcohol and possibly even drugs. She also let them know what she had been hearing about Trevor and how he mistreated girls.

Her parents were horrified, but they set their horror aside for a moment and sprang into action. They looked up Samantha's address and took off for the house, afraid of what they might find when they got there. Dani stayed at home and went up to her room after they left so she could think and pray about the situation. She was glad that everything was finally coming to light, because she had been so worried about Drew. But she was also worried that Drew would never forgive her for telling their parents what had been going on. Dani knew that now more than ever before, her sister needed her prayers and her support.

Bonfire blazing, people laughing and milling around the yard, Drew and Trevor were having a great time being silly and raucous by the fire. One thing Drew noticed about alcohol was that it made her less inhibited. Things that would have made her uncomfortable just a few hours before suddenly became completely acceptable and desirable. She became very comfortable with Trevor's touches and even initiated some herself, which made him very happy.

After an hour or so of flirting around the fire, Trevor wanted Drew to come with him to find a private place for a few minutes. She knew that it would mean more kissing; and even though she was scared, she really wanted to go. They decided that the pool shed would be a great place for them to hang out. On their way to the pool shed, Drew heard something funny coming from the front of the house. Wondering what was happening, she pulled Trevor toward the front, even though he was trying to pull her in the direction of the shed.

When she got a little closer, she heard shouting. "Where is my daughter? Someone better bring me to her *now!*"

Drew instantly recognized her father's voice and turned to Trevor, hoping he could help her make sense of it all. Her mind was fuzzy because of the alcohol and drugs, so she couldn't fully grasp what was happening to her—and she even started giggling.

Trevor shot her a look and said, "This really isn't funny."

"Everything's funny." Drew giggled again. She was completely incapable of grasping the gravity of the situation. "I know what I'll do. I'm going in to the bathroom so I can clean myself up before I see them." She ran off through the back entrance to find the bathroom before her parents found her.

In the bright yellow bathroom, Drew took a look in the mirror over the sink. She was horrified by what she saw. Her clothes were a mess, her makeup was smeared, and she knew that she reeked of smoke—cigarette and bonfire smoke. As soon as she thought of the smoking, her stomach began to turn. The combination of beer and smoke on an empty stomach were quickly becoming too much for her to handle. As the bubbling continued to rise in her belly, she turned and lunged for the toilet, emptying the contents of her stomach. Feeling a bit better, she washed her face and hands and tried to smooth her hair. Wishing she could stall a little longer, she knew that her time was up. It was time to face the music.

She slowly opened the door a crack. She had no idea what she would say to her mom and dad. She realized that she had disappointed them in just about every possible way in that one night. As she was coming to her senses and remembering everything about the night and what led up to it, Drew wished with all her heart that she could go back and have another chance to do things the right way. But it was too late.

She saw her parents enter the house and approach Sam's sister, who pointed toward the bathroom. They both saw her at the same time, and there was a moment of eye contact that Drew would never forget. Her mom was crying and wiping her eyes. She looked so sad. Her dad mostly looked mad. Drew wasn't sure which one she was dreading the most: the disappointment or the anger.

Drew started to open her mouth to speak, but Dad cut her off and said, "I'm not interested in hearing anything from you right now, Drew. Just collect your things and let's go."

Mom covered her mouth with her tissue and sobbed harder when she heard her husband's words.

Drew quietly got her jacket from the hook on the back of the door. She started the long, shameful walk out to the car and couldn't lift her head to look her parents in the eye. They said nothing.

She sat in the backseat, silent, alone, listening to her mom crying softly in the front seat. Suddenly her words came back to her, haunting her: *"I've got everything under control."* She regretted those words so much. But it was too late. She had failed.

Dad started to walk back into the house to talk to Samantha but decided he would be better off taking his daughter home and coming back. As her dad walked to his car door, Drew caught a glimpse of Trevor standing on the side of the house, watching the scene unfold. He shook his head in disgust; he looked angry. For a brief moment, Drew felt a bit of shock to realize that he was angry with her instead of being worried about her. She shrugged off those feelings, because she had much more important things to deal with.

Her dad got into the car, backed out of the driveway, and headed down the street. Before they got to the end of the block, they heard sirens and saw lights flashing. Three police cars screamed past them and pulled into the driveway they had just left. Policemen got out of the car with their hands on their guns and started shouting at people in the yard.

Dad continued driving away, but they all realized immediately what could have happened if they had arrived five minutes later than they had. That realization dissolved Drew into tears. She knew she deserved to be there facing the police with her "friends," but she was so glad that she wasn't.

A few minutes later, at home, the Danielses all walked into the house; and Drew, feeling sick again, ran to the bathroom. After she was sick for the second time, she decided to take a quick shower to attempt to rid herself of the filth that covered her from the evening. She stood in the shower, under the hot water for a long time. It was difficult to hurry, because the room seemed to be swaying. She finally finished and got dressed.

"Mom. . .Dad. . ." She didn't know what to say to them when she entered the family room. They were sitting silently in the dimly lit room, not even speaking to each other.

"Drew, I honestly don't know if we have it in us to talk to you about this tonight." Dad had his head in his hands and he wouldn't look at her. Drew's mom stared blankly at her, almost as though she didn't even know her. Perhaps she felt that she didn't.

"Please. . .I need to. . .I can't leave it until tomorrow. . .we need to fix this." Drew begged for their attention, because the thought of having to wait until tomorrow to face them was too much for her.

"Drew, there is no quick fix for this. And it really doesn't matter what you need right now. Your mom and I just don't have it in us to figure out what we want to say or need to say to you. It's going to take time. And you're just going to have to deal with that."

Drew hung her head in sadness and embarrassment, knowing that she had really crushed her parents and destroyed their trust in her. She would do anything for the chance to take back her actions that evening. But that wasn't going to happen. The only thing for her to do was to go to bed.

"I'm so sorry. I love you both. Good night."

"We love you, too, Drew. Good night."

Climbing into her bed, Drew was careful not to wake Dani, who was in her own bed across the room, pretending to be asleep. Dani lay there, afraid that Drew would be mad at her for all she had told their parents, so she didn't let on that she was awake.

Drew lay in bed for a long time as tears quietly soaked her pillow. So much had died that night. It was the death of her innocence in many ways. It was the death of her parents' trust in her. It was the death of her faith in people. It was the death of her faith in herself. She knew that somehow she would have to find a way to resurrect her faith in God before any of those things could be restored.

Chapter 13

TRUTH AND CONSEQUENCES

Drew woke up slowly the morning after the party. She rolled over, nauseous, and forgot for a moment why she felt sick. Suddenly, memories from the night before started coming back to her. With a loud groan, she turned over and covered her head with her pillow, trying to escape the memories, even for just one more moment.

After narrowly escaping a run-in with the police, Drew felt equal amounts of regret and relief. She was so regretful about the things she had done, and she knew there were consequences for them that she still had to face. But she was also so very relieved that she escaped a legal problem. Also, as difficult as it was for her to admit to herself, she was relieved that she had been found out. It was too stressful to carry on like she had been. It was just not natural for her to lie to her parents; and, looking back on the night before, she didn't like the person she had been. Plus, she knew that she had really been in over her head and was headed for some real trouble. Who knew what last night would have led to after alcohol and drugs. . .she could have done anything. And it was beginning to seem like Trevor knew that and had been happily taking advantage of it.

Drew sat up in bed and looked over at her sister. Dani was lying on her side with her eyes open, looking back at Drew.

"I'm so sorry," Dani whispered.

"Why are you sorry?" Drew was confused.

"I totally ratted you out. I told them everything I knew and everything I suspected. I'd just had enough with worrying about you all on my own, and I thought I was doing the right thing."

"You did do the right thing, and you have nothing to be sorry for."

"Drew, what happened last night? Were there really drugs and alcohol at that party? You didn't do any, did you? Please tell me you didn't." Dani had so many questions for Drew.

"I wish I could tell you that I did nothing wrong, but I can't. Everything you heard about the party was true. I wish I could say that I was strong and didn't do any of it, but I'm so embarrassed to admit, I did it all."

"Drew! Seriously? Why? I'm so bummed. I mean. . .I just wish this hadn't happened at all. I should have stopped it somehow. What did Mom and Dad say?"

"Slow down, sis. It's not your fault, and there was nothing you could have done to stop it. It was my choice and my fault. And believe me, I wish it hadn't happened, too. As for Mom and Dad, we haven't even talked about it yet. I guess it's about time for me to go face the music. Stalling isn't going to help things a bit."

Drew got out of bed, leaving Dani to think over all she had just heard. She brushed her teeth and washed her face, stopping to look at herself for a minute. As she stared at her reflection, she just couldn't figure out how things had gotten so far out of hand. She tied her hair back into a ponytail and went downstairs. Her mom was in the kitchen, making coffee, and her dad was sitting at the table. The night's sleep and the fresh light of day seemed to have calmed them a bit, so she took a seat with her dad and waited for someone to say something. No one did.

"Mom, Dad, I can't tell you how sorry I am. I really screwed up. But I can honestly tell you that I'm relieved to have it over. It was really getting out of hand, and I felt kind of trapped. . . you know, in over my head."

"Oh, Drew. Where did we go wrong? What should we have done differently to teach you better about right and wrong? We thought we were doing all the right things," Mom said, crying.

"Mom, you have done a fantastic job. Look at Dani. I'm just different. I'm more stubborn. And I guess I have to learn from my own mistakes, which is part of being stubborn— but it's not your fault. I have learned so much from all of this. I mean, I know that I'll be punished, but believe me, there is no punishment that could be worse than how I feel already. I never knew what real regret felt like. I know I've hurt you. . .that just kills me."

"Oh, Drew, this is so far beyond punishment." Dad fingered the corner of his unread newspaper. "Yes, there will be consequences, but it's more than that. We need to change the way we do things around here. You've lost our trust, and it's going to take a long time to earn that back. And," Dad continued, "just so you understand, it's not that we want to withhold our trust as a punishment, it's just that we can't let go of you right now for fear of what you'll do to yourself. We're going to have to keep you really close for a long time."

"I understand, Dad. I don't blame you. Whatever you want or need from me, whatever I can do, I will do gladly. I am just so grateful to have been spared what a lot of my friends probably faced last night, and I'm so relieved to have been saved from myself and from what I might have done."

"Drew, you're going to need to step down from cheerleading," her mom said without looking at her.

Tears sprang to Drew's eyes. "Oh, Mom, I was so afraid you'd say that. Is that really necessary? I mean, it's a school-sponsored activity. . . wait. . .you're right. I just got finished saying that I would do whatever it took. If you think it's important, I won't question you."

Dad sat up in his chair. "Now, Drew, that tells me that you are serious in your remorse. Thank you for that. But yes, it's important. For one thing, we don't want you associating with those kids anymore. For another thing, we feel that you need to get your focus off of yourself, your looks, and the attention and all that comes with cheerleading and get back to basics like school and good friends."

"Okay, Dad. I can understand that."

"As for the rest of your punishment, it's just that things are going to change. No more staying out with friends. No sleepovers, no trips to the mall. You're going to go to school and come home. You and your sister can find your relationship again. You can go to church and youth group activities. But that's about it." Mr. Daniels held up his hand. "Before you ask, I don't know how long. I guess until we feel you are safe from yourself and your poor decisions."

Drew sat with her head down. It was difficult to look her parents in the eye, so she just took in their words.

"Drew, your dad and I really want to encourage you to get some counseling from one of the pastors at church. We'd like to see you get back to your roots and find your faith in God again. I think you've seen that you don't have everything under control. Perhaps you've realized that you need Him to be in control. They can help you let go and let Him in again."

"Okay, Mom. I'll do it. It's a good idea." Drew was trying to stop crying, but she was overcome with emotion. Regret mingled with relief was a powerful emotion.

"As for today," Dad said, "I have some things I want you to do around the house. Some yard work and some other projects that will keep you busy and give you time to think. Fair?"

"Fair," Drew agreed.

"One more thing, Drew." Her mom paused and collected her thoughts. "I don't want this conversation to end without making sure that you know how much your dad and I love you. This doesn't change that one bit. We love you so much that we aren't going to let you go down this path that you've found. We don't think you're a terrible person, and our love for you hasn't changed. We know that you've made some mistakes, and we're going to do our best to make sure it doesn't happen again."

Drew nodded as the tears fell hard on her lap.

"Also," Mom continued, "God's love for you hasn't changed a bit, either. He has begun a good work in your life; He began that work a long time ago. And the Bible promises in Philippians 1:6 that when He begins that good work in someone, He will carry it on to completion. He'll finish what He started in you. You just need to let go of the control and let Him be your Lord and Savior. You know what I mean?"

Drew nodded, still unable to talk. Her mom went to her immediately and put her motherly arms around her and held her until she could compose herself.

"I love you both. And I heard everything you said about letting God back into the driver's seat in my life. I will figure out how to do that. I want Him to finish His work in me."

The day passed quickly. Drew was surprised at how good it felt to work hard. She raked leaves, cleaned out the gutters, stacked wood, and organized the garage and the basement. She worked until she was sweating, and it was like a form of therapy. Dani helped her for a little while—not that Drew needed the help, but they needed the time together. As each project got completed, it felt like a piece of the broken puzzle of her life was put back together. Each time she moved on to the next project, she left a piece of the pain behind.

The one dark moment was when her dad came to tell her what had happened the night before, after they left. The police arrested everyone. Most of them got charged with underage drinking, others got charged with providing alcohol to minors or buying it with a fake ID. Several even got arrested for possession and/or use of drugs. Sorrow for her friends washed over her, but it was mingled, once again, with relief. Neither Drew nor her dad had any idea if this would mean jail time for any of them or if they would face suspension or expulsion from school. The fact that Drew could have easily been with them continued to fill her with immense relief even though she was so sad for her friends.

"Remember, Drew, real friends wouldn't have put you in a situation like that. They would have known that you weren't ready and that it was unsafe and illegal. Those types of kids aren't the kinds of friends you want. Do you realize that? Really?"

"Yeah, Dad. I mean, it's hard to let go of what I thought was a dream come true. But I see what you're saying, and I agree. I miss my old friends. You know? Girls who made me a better person, made it easy to be who I am instead of making me work so hard to be who they wanted me to be."

"Ah, yes. I do think you get it, honey. That's exactly what I was hoping you'd realize." He gave her a little hug and then left her to finish her project.

Drew looked forward to going to church. She knew that she needed some spiritual healing. But she dreaded seeing the looks on people's faces and wondering if they knew the story. Oh well, she had to face everyone sooner or later.

Pastor Michaels was his usual fiery self. He was finishing up his series about control, and his sermon focused on how people need to let the attractive things of the world fade into the background rather than let them control desires and drive ambition.

"God doesn't value the things that the world does," Pastor Michaels taught. "Popularity, looks, human ability, and material things mean nothing to Him. In fact, the Bible tells us that people who want those things more than they want God's will already have their reward. That means that whatever you focus on is your reward. If your only goal is to get the most you can out of life, then your reward *is* this life. But if your goal is to love and serve God and you follow Him, then your reward comes from Him.

"The Bible says that where your heart is, there your treasure will be also. So, if your heart is set on the things of earth that fade and rust away, then you have shown Him where your treasure is. But if your heart is set on things above—God's will, showing His love to others, learning from and living the scriptures—then you will be showing God and the world where your treasure is. There is no mistaking it. You can't serve both God and the world.

"Just remember, all that glitters loses its luster in the light of God's glory. Let your heart and mind and all you desire be illuminated by the influence of God, not the temporary sparkle that the world offers."

Drew took in the words of the message that she felt was directed toward her. She decided once again that all that glittered was not what she wanted, and that He had everything under control.

My Decision

I, *(include your name here)*, have read the story of Drew Daniels and have learned from the choices that she made and the consequences that she faced. I promise to think before I act and, in all things, to choose God's will over mine. Specifically, I will honor my parents and avoid situations that include alcohol and drugs. I will also protect my purity by not sneaking around with boys and doing things that I have to hide from my parents.

Please pray the following prayer:

Father God, I know that I don't know everything, and I can't possibly have everything under control. Please help me remember the lessons I've learned as I've read this book. Help me to honor my parents and serve You by making right choices and avoiding questionable situations. It is my desire to avoid alcohol, drugs, and physical intimacy as I grow up. Help me to avoid situations that present those things as options to me. And if I find myself in a tight spot, please help me find a way out and give me the strength to take it. I know that You have everything under control, so I submit to Your will. Amen.

Congratulations on your decision! Please sign this contract signifying your commitment. Have someone you trust, like a parent or a pastor, witness your choice.

_____

Signed

_____

Witnessed by

→ CHECK IT OUT

For information on the latest
Scenarios books, great giveways, girl talk,
and more, visit scenariosforgirls.com!

Find Scenarios author
Nicole O'Dell on the Web:

Web site: www.nicoleodell.com
Facebook: facebook.com/nicoleodell
Twitter: twitter.com/Nicole_Odell
Blog: nicoleodell.blogspot.com

Teen Talk Radio, with host Nicole O'Dell,
airs on www.choicesradio.com.

SCENARIOS FOR GIRLS

RISKY BUSINESS

Molly Jacobs gets hired at the ultimate girls' clothing store and her friends—even the popular girls in school—are envious. Kate Walker secures a spot on her school's swim team but soon becomes obsessed—with practice and making it through the championships with flying colors. What happens when Molly and Kate are faced with making difficult choices? How will they handle the risky business?

SWEPT AWAY

Seniors and best friends, Amber and Brittany, are neck and neck in a good-natured competition for a car being given away by a local business. Sophomore Lilly Armstrong is always looking for ways to escape the confines of her unhappy home. What happens when Amber and Lilly are faced with making difficult choices?

Available wherever books are sold.